SILVER DOLLAR SOLDIER

SUSAN ETZEL VIZE

BALBOA.PRESS

A DIVISION OF HAY HOUSE

Balboa Press books may be ordered through booksellers or by contacting:

Balboa Press
A Division of Hay House
1663 Liberty Drive
Bloomington, IN 47403
www.balboapress.com
844-682-1282

Print information available on the last page.

ISBN: 978-1-9822-6661-5 (sc)
ISBN: 978-1-9822-6663-9 (hc)
ISBN: 978-1-9822-6662-2 (e)

Library of Congress Control Number: 2021906668

Balboa Press rev. date: 05/10/2021

CONTENTS

DEDICATION

To Dad,

A member of the Greatest Generation,
With love and respect

INTRODUCTION

The 371st Engineer Construction Battalion was commissioned to prepare the way before combat troops by building facilities, roads, and bridges and then destroying the same resources after use in order to thwart German forces. Although, they were trained to fight if need be, their primary mission was essential support. This Battalion consisted of three companies and Headquarters (HQ). Private First Class Jean Etzel was assigned to Company A, Platoon 2.

The Army Engineers were recruited from families of carpenters and mechanics. PFC Etzel came from a family of both. His job description on his discharge papers indicate his primary assignment was to the motor pool as a chauffeur although he assisted with carpentry, construction and demolition as well. He served in Northern France, the Ardennes, Rhineland, and Central Europe. The Army recognized his service with 3 Overseas Service Bars, European Campaign Medal with 4 Bronze Battle Stars, the Good Conduct Medal, and the World War II Victory Medal. He was drafted into the army as an 18 year old high school graduate in September of 1943 and honorably discharged three years later just shy of his 21st birthday.

German troops crossed the Polish border on September 1, 1939, in a long and daring Nazi attempt, under Adolph Hitler's reign of the Third Reich, to control the world. In England, Neville Chamberlain's cabinet refused to retire until he issued an ultimatum, which he finally did the morning of September 3, 1939, calling for German troops to be withdrawn within two hours. When they were not, Chamberlain declared war. The French joined the effort later that day after an ultimatum that expired at 5:00 p.m.

Although the Poles tried to fight back, they were unprepared for the German invasion. Worse still, the Soviets entered Poland from the east on the premise of protecting their own White Russians. By October 5, the Germans and Russians had taken 900,000 Polish soldiers captive. Although 70,000 escaped, over 20% of the Polish population died in the brutal assaults on their country. The rest of the world watched, appalled, as Hitler began plans to invade France "to decide the domination of Europe." World War II in Photographs-David Boyle

Induction

Jean came into the world during the Roaring Twenties in an era of flappers, illegal booze, parties and good times, until the prosperity ended suddenly with the Crash on October 29, 1929, and not just the US, but the whole globe entered the Great Depression. Growing up dirt poor, the youngest in a family of ten children, he managed to have a happy childhood. He entered World War II in 1943, just after high school

When Jean got drafted into the war in 1943, he was 18, standing about 5' 10" and weighing around 165. His thin frame, topped with straggly, reddish brown hair, highlighted his freckles and his impish grin, below his deep set dancing eyes, a modern day Tom Sawyer, with the adventures and experiences to prove it. By the time he returned home in 1946, he was 21, stood 6'2" and weighed 195. He carried himself differently, almost gliding onto the stairs of the porch, his uniform crisp and his hat held in his hand. His own mother had to look twice when he arrived on their doorstep after those three years which had made him a man, one of the Iron Youth, as teen soldiers had been called in World War I.

The day he left had held an eerie aura of the finality of his innocence as he bid his mother and father goodbye on that same porch. He was their baby, the youngest of ten.

"You're not ready," his mother said, but Jean stood quietly, not wanting to argue with her.

Silent moments passed. After having been denied once for poor eyesight, he had received a new induction notice and he held it out for them to peruse for perhaps the third time. Nothing had changed. His orders were still the same: report for duty. Yet his parents' hesitancy over having close to an empty nest still hung in the air on this day he must leave.

Long minutes passed before Jean, sensing that something had palpably changed, saw a look of resignation in his father's eyes. He took Jean aside, and slipped a silver dollar into his palm, pressing it flat against the flesh of his hand.

"For luck," the tired, hard-working man, who had borne the absence of three other sons to the war, said softly. Jean turned the coin over and noted it was from 1925, the year of his birth. His eyes told his father more thanks than his lips could muster the courage to speak as the two grappled with the goodbye.

With great difficulty Jean moved to the small, resolute woman beside his father. She had already given him a St. Christopher medal. His mother, ever stoic, her intelligent eyes misting, went to him quickly, took him in her arms for a brief, almost tearless, but fierce hug. After a straightening of his lapel, smoothed down with the flat of her hand, she turned away abruptly, her voice catching on a sob. Jean held her hand a second or two before she pulled completely from him, turning her face, not wanting to have him see her cry. Then Jean shook hands with his father, who had a carpenter's hand, well worn and rough, but loving, the silky feel of the silver between their fingers, a bond between them. The image of his parents bolstering each other on the porch of his childhood home in Rock Island, IL stayed seared into his mind throughout the journey of his life.

Jean got lucky with his assignment for basic training. Jean's first new acquaintance was Jack Pemberton from Kewanee, some 45 minutes from his hometown. Jack and he merged into the seats on the train as the new recruits processed into the Army, traveling with little gear, but much baggage on the Rock Island Lines, whose long, lonely and mournful whistle he had grown up hearing deep into the night.

Jean next met Red, an energetic and superbly funny young man with hair the color of an Irish setter. "Uncle Sam's been saving this seat for you, young men," Red said to Jean and Jack as they worked their way sideways down the aisle. Red pointed to the empty places beside him.

Red then introduced him to Ernie Allen, a studious, slightly older type, originally from Chicago, who still appreciated a good laugh. "I've got room above my seat for your duffel," Ernie invited, "and here's another for a card game," Allen pointed to a boyish faced guy with curly black hair called Mikey, from rural Southern Illinois, his seat mate, and their fifth game player, bringing him into the conversation. Soon they all had told pieces of their similar and dissimilar backgrounds, and a friendly rapport allowed them to converse quietly as they played Euchre, or to sit in comfortable silence as the train glided into the city of Chicago, huge with metallic skylines, and the bustle of big city life.

Red wanted to bet on the cards, but the other four compromised at pennies for each hand. The red-head's laughter came often as he won most of the hands.

"You're not cheating, are you?" Mikey asked with an elbow to Red's ribs, and Red jostled him back. "My family raises horses," Mikey said. "We can smell fraudulence."

"Does that smell like manure?" Jack asked with a straight face

"If you think I'm cheatin', prove it," Red challenged with a laugh.

"I don't think anybody'd cheat over a few pennies," said Ernie good naturedly.

"We'll see when we get down to the end of our pennies," Jean cracked, as they continued to play, not cheat, and watch Red keep winning.

Following a long, rumbling train ride, that allowed those traveling to the same destination, plenty of time to ruminate or get to know one another, the nervous men, many of them as young as Jean, finally arrived for their induction, in Chicago, the Windy City, Carl Sandburg's hog butchering capital of the world.

Disengaging from the train, the five stuck together for the duration of the "hurry up and wait" line in the tallest building any of them had ever seen. Jean and the others endured the endless wait, the long roll calls. They did the expected paperwork, and received the necessary injections, haircuts, inspections of eyes and teeth, and other bodily parts which everyone hated, all experiences that solidified their imposed choices to be soldiers and their answer to the call. That introduction period in Chicago led them to the next step. After a whirlwind look at the city of Chicago, led by Ernie, they boarded another train southward bound.

While his eldest brother Larry had been sent to Texas, and brothers Norb and George based on the west coast, Jean's orders eventually sent him only a couple of hours from his home, to Camp Ellis, Illinois, located just outside of Macomb. His military training, because of its close proximity, would allow him the opportunity to hitch a ride home to Rock Island on long weekends.

The base in that flat, farmland area near the Spoon River began with tents erected in late winter rains that made the ground muddy, and huddling through the storms and dirtied snow, made them miserable. As the weather changed, so did the camp, with full-fledged preparations of the ground for the construction of real buildings.

The barren expanse of land became their home, forged with the bonds of friendship and young men working together to create a space, their own space, a space to live in, and to learn how to become a soldier, to become a man. The cold overpowered them and yet, at night, in the warmth of the campfires after the day was done, being together with a common goal overcame their dreary days of fighting the temperatures, and of defeating the weather. They had time to work, eat, converse, play cards and dice or darts, sleep, and build community. The whole experience defined the storm of their new lives. Eventually the tents turned into wooden barracks, buildings that became the hallmark of their growth.

The completely disciplined way of life did not differ all that much from his routine at home being the youngest of six living children fighting for a place in the family. All the soldiers learned the basics of life, now called the Army: combat and survival techniques, rifle training, cleaning of guns, together with the everyday care of uniforms, making bed sheets snap, and adapting to their new life which kept them busy in their first home away from home.

Following orders, learning military maneuvers, picking up the lingo of the service, the expectations of the sergeants, and helping maintain morale kept Jean alert, occupied as he was with blending in with the rest of his peers. Most of these youngsters fell into bed in the evenings, exhausted by the physical work of getting in shape to march and to survive who knew what the next day. Chow time consisted of fighting for one's share of the food, with soldiers sparring to get someone else's meal by passing gas, picking their nose, or telling stories about vomit or manure. Those who couldn't manage to ignore the attacks against civility sometimes went hungry.

One early incident left a deep impression on Jean, as a burly man, with the hairiest arms he'd ever seen, turned his head sideways, snorted several times, put his finger against his nostril, then shot a wad of snot into the aisle way between tables, making at least two men lose their lunches, while the rest laughed uproariously. Naturally, the unused portion of both lunches did not go to waste.

Oftentimes there were scuffles, and even fights while waiting in line, or reaching for bread being passed around. The last piece, even the heel, got snatched easily. Though the food was sparse, it wasn't without flavor, but eating always made Jean homesick.

"Lights out" meant being considerate of others in the barracks, even if sleep didn't come, and roll call always came early just as it had in Rock Island, only without the benevolent hovering of his mother over his breakfast.

The one thing Jean did not know quite how to contend with involved several questions about his given name, some humorous and some not so, as almost everyone who saw his name spelled out asked him why he had a girl's name.

"Hey, Jean, what's with your name?" A lanky Yankee, originally from the east coast, teased him in a strange dialect. The man grinned, but his tone made Jean uneasy. He had heard this question before, and knew he would hear it again. Jean would nod or wave his hand in dismissal, and ignore the attempts to rattle him.

Yank persisted. "C'mon then, tell me how you got yer name."

"My parents chose it," Jean replied.

"Well, they must have had a reason."

"They liked it," Jean retorted.

"Good enough," Yank retreated with a smile.

These new and quickly made friendships took Jean by surprise, as, being the baby in his family and probably spoiled, as most of his siblings claimed, he gradually saw that telling the truth garnered the best response. He had handled being teased before. That honest insight came to him one evening as he settled onto his cot preparing to sleep, but feeling homesick for the days of his childhood home, and his family who loved him. He tossed and turned on the narrow bed, and could not get comfortable. Yawning, he punched his pillow into shape, turned over, and pushed his face into the softness, as drowsiness finally took him.

His parents had argued over his name. His father had wanted John, after his wife's brother, his good friend, but for some reason, his mother insisted that she did not want that name. All of their other nine children had been named for the saint on whose day they had been born. Four of the ten had already died, two infant boys, Fred and Jamie, and an infant girl, Maryanne, called Billie, and one girl, Frances, otherwise known as Sis, who passed at age12 from diphtheria, probably coughing up her vocal chords, or so the doctor told them.

These losses fostered more than the usual coddling of their other children as Jean's parents fought to provide better than the grave for the remaining six. In a time of economic hardship, with the mere daily duty of providing food, clothing, and shelter, Fred and Maryanne wrangled with the name as if the meaning might mark the difference between life and death.

The priest finally intervened, suggesting they name him Jean, the French form of John. Happily, his baptism began with this compromise, and the infant, officially christened Jean, made his entry into a community of Catholic faith and family, a rather small, but warm and close church family that cast its concern over him almost as carefully as his parents.

Not much had escaped his mother's watchful eye as he grew. Maryanne, the motherly disciplinarian, who had birthed him at the age of 40 in their own home, kept a fine line between acceptable and unacceptable behavior as she raised her children through the late years of the prosperous Roaring Twenties, the subsequent Crash of the stock market, and the all encompassing Great Depression. Demanding they do their best in school, she helped them with her sharp intelligence and keen attention to detail, insisting that knowledge was power, and power was preparedness.

Jean's life had revolved around family, school, chores at home, and adventures with his family, and then later, his friends. As a young lad, he and his eldest brother Larry waited daily for his grandfather to come home from work. Eddie always saved cookies for them as they met up on the street corner, and red-haired Irish Eddie, speaking in a soft Irish brogue, clasped up the young Jean, twirling him around before setting him down and walking hand in hand to the duplex where they all lived. Jean could hear the lilting Irish words dancing from his grandfather's lips, trailing into his memory: "I'll be after...."

After Jean started school, which he did not like due to the fact that he was often bored, or compared unfairly to his older siblings, especially Norb, the lone wolf who almost always had his nose in a book, and Catherine, his A student sister, his mother made him sweep, do yard work, and run errands for her. He liked being out in the fresh air better, hiking up his short pants, handed down to him from one of his older siblings, and letting his imagination run with him as he completed the tasks set before him.

Sister Annelle told him he had an imagination, a good one, but that he needed to learn to spell. He knew that, but couldn't understand the need for dates in history, or the exact precision required for writing. He liked to be creative. He preferred to go his own way, and he hated being expected to perform academically as his siblings did. He was, after all, himself.

Jean also learned to stand up for himself with four older brothers: Larry, Tom, George, and Norb, always telling him what to do, and where he could not go, which was usually wherever they were going. He relished the times they would let him tag along, and felt their approval in their unspoken support of him, in the pleasure they took in his antics.

Norb often walked with him and Catherine to school, and they usually followed at a safe distance behind this next oldest brother, the only one who dared talk back to their mother, as he carved out his niche in the family as the one most likely to succeed at getting his own way. Norb and George once had a fight in the backyard near the garage, and George picked up a baseball bat and started pounding on the door in frustration. Jean called for his dad to come mediate just as a loud rumbling noise broke through the din of his brothers yelling at each other. Jean and his dad arrived just in time to see the collapsed garage door close in on itself.

Fred put his hand to his head, scratching in consternation. "Now see what you've gone and done? I'm going to have to fix that now."

"Well, I knew you didn't want me pounding on Norb, and he started it." George said reasonably.

Jean also always associated Norb with the long white underwear he draped over the end of his bed, which, when Jean sometimes woke at night, scared him with its ghostly legs flapping in the summer wind, in tune to the howls of the breeze, making Jean believe their bedroom had been invaded by spirits.

His sister Catherine, three years older, the only living girl-child, kept a practiced eye on his escapades in the neighborhood, his companion in kick the can, kickball, and catching fireflies. Jean and Catherine often played together, left behind by the other, older siblings, off on one adventure after another, riding their bicycles late into the soft breezy summer nights. Sometimes on those nights, none of them got home until almost midnight where they slipped inside an unlocked door for a bedtime snack, and a hug goodnight from one or both of their parents.

Plenty of other children, including their cousins, helped keep the summer fun, and if all else failed, someone would get up a game of "Red Rover, Red Rover" before settling down to playing marbles which made the late afternoons scoot away. On summer-lit nights Jean often watched Tom work on the family cars, changing oil, checking spark plugs, and the batteries on the old Model T, which they kept in perfect running condition.

In the winters they built elaborate snow forts, had snowball fights, shoveled walks for money to go to the movies for a quarter apiece, and made igloos almost as warm as their houses. Tom often invited Jean into the garage on those colder evenings to learn something new about the way their car engine worked. They would spend hours under the hood, cleaning the parts. They never lacked for something to do. They were never bored. If they said they were bored, they knew Maryanne would tell them what work needed doing.

Her husband Fred, a practical builder, more easy going, managed somehow to keep things together even when he could not find regular work as a carpenter. He hunted for jobs, using his contacts, and a sense of humor to wheedle projects from friends of friends. Even during the actual Depression, he eventually managed to build a house for a hard working woman of some means who promised him the money when he finished. In good faith, taking another's word as bond, Fred completed the structure from the ground up, even building the precise cabinetry from scratch, and she paid him, taking a photograph of him and Jean holding the check for $3,000 outside her home, finished in 1939, the year "Wizard of Oz" debuted on the silver screen.

In 1941 his mother had been the first to ride in a car over the recently constructed Centennial Bridge, a structure connecting Rock Island, Illinois with Davenport, Iowa. This project, his brother George, an engineering firm supervisor, helped oversee, often taking Jean to watch as the bridge took shape, spanning the Mississippi in spurts of growth silhouetted against the twilight sky. Jean had been impressed by the camaraderie of the team constructing the monumental tie between two states, a bridge eliminating the need for ferries to cross over the Mississippi in the warmer weather, and brave souls to walk over the iced river in winter.

Jean had seen photographs of men and women walking across the iced over Mississippi in winter, and he marveled that this new bridge connected two states, Illinois and Iowa.

George had also taken Jean on his rounds sometimes when he worked as a Merchant Policeman, protecting the individually owned stores on Mill Street, carrying a gun proudly, and bringing it home with him to hang on the hook by the back door where, one evening, having left the safety off, George accidentally nudged the firearm, while hanging up his coat, and it went off suddenly, frightening the whole family. After that, Maryanne insisted he keep it in the car or on the back porch.

Jean's second oldest brother Tom worked in the produce section of a nearby family owned grocery store on Mill Street. When he wasn't making deliveries to the notorious gangster, John Looney, in his mansion on the hill of 20th Street, and wondering if he'd run into gunfire, Tom did more mundane tasks. Each day he sorted through the fruits and vegetables, separating those pieces with bruises and softened flesh bursting from his touch. The limp, rusting vegetables showing signs of decay, Tom removed from the good produce. His boss, knowing that Tom came from a large family, told Tom to keep what they would have ordinarily thrown out, and to take the almost spoiled food home.

Maryanne carefully cut away the bad spots and made rich, aromatic sauces from the ripened fruits, or wove them skillfully into cake or breads when she could get enough flour, butter and sugar. The vegetables, cleaned and trimmed of wilt, she threw into a simmering pot of water, seasoned with all manner of spices and flavored with an elaborately bare meat bone about to be discarded by the butcher. This combination soup/stew, enhanced with potatoes, noodles, or rice and barley, when they had them, made a hearty supper, filling, and healthy during the hard, lean times of the Depression. Except for the turnips. Jean couldn't stand the turnips. Or the rutabagas.

Jean passed these off under his chair, to Rum Dum, his beloved cat, because one of Jean's chores was to clean his litter box and keep him fed and watered. The vegetables seemed to keep the cat regular. This feline, like most other cats with that fascinatingly ambivalent nature, allowed the family to care for him, but Jean was his special person. Jean had tamed the creature. Experimenting with a scissors one day, Jean had cut off the cat's whiskers not realizing that the whiskers allowed the animal to measure his ability to maneuver through small spaces.

After months passed, the whiskers grew back and the family had moved from a too small home, to a slightly larger space, but Rum Dum kept returning to the previous house out of habit. Sadly, Jean believed Rum Dum blamed him for the unfortunate shave and felt betrayed. Eventually the family asked a former neighbor to keep a lookout and feed the lost kitty.

But Jean never forgot the cat, which sometimes returned to the new home on the cold winter nights when Jean happily wrapped his arms around the sleek, soft fur, breathing in the rhythm of the regular breath of another living thing with a regular heartbeat, and a soft purr that sounded like a well oiled motor, a being closer to him than his brothers or sister.

Jean stirred on his cot, rubbing his eyes sleepily, missing that small bundle of fur that had slipped to the surface of his dream. That cat had been the symbol of his childhood security, much the same as he supposed the silver dollar in his pocket and his St. Christopher medal would take him through the war. In a way, Jean now understood how the cat felt about wanting to return to his original home, the hauntingly familiar place calling to him from the sleepy mist he tried to shake off. When the bugle for roll call sounded again, and he slipped out of his blanket, his bare feet touching the cold wooden floor, then he was fully awake.

Camp Ellis and
Building Bridges

ebruary 3, 1944 marked the beginning of an entirely new
concept in basic training with the gradual reorganization
of the 371st Engineers into four companies near LaSalle,
Illinois: A, B, C, and D under the temporary command of Colonel
Adcock, whose name alone brought more than a few bawdy jokes
and under the breath one-liners from the men and boys of his
watch. Red, with the Irish Setter hair, standing near Jean said
something about Moby Dick in a sea faring sort of dialect which
set the others to snorting. Ernie and Mikey, and then Jack and
Yank followed up with variations on the theme, along with many
others muttering under their muffled breaths, until the rattled
Colonel flushed with anger at his loss of control.

Who could blame them, when the sole pleasure of each day
consisted of soldiers planning their evening's activities in the
nearby city? Into this mix of chaos and good humor, Jean and
the other new recruits from Chicago finally settled in at Camp
Ellis. The place never lacked for amusement of some sort. Nights

especially brought them together in the barracks to read mail, share family pictures, or, even better, photos of sweethearts, and to tell stories about their former escapades back home.

Ernie kept a notebook of information about the 5 W's: who, what, when, where, and why. He often pulled one or more of the soldiers aside to pick their brains on names and places he would write into his chronicles, and then he would read what he wrote for their amusement. Ernie had a dream of being a reporter or a teacher. He was married and had a child, a little boy. "At least my name will live on if I don't come back," Ernie said, as he jotted in his journal.

"Quit," Mikey said. "Let's not even go there."

"We'll go where they send us, and we will like it," Red said in a staccato voice much like one of the officers spoke, and the others recognized it immediately, laughing at the good impression.

"Wherever you go, there you are," Jean said in an innocent, schoolboy voice, similar to the cadence of "Which Way Did He Go, George?" in the old cartoon, and then slapped his knee, and began laughing, a loud, infectious chortle.

Sometimes things seem funnier when soldiers feel tired, hungry, and unsure of what tomorrow will bring, and the others grinned, then began laughing too, at his silly remark. Jean had a great laugh, a contagious laugh. They laughed with him.

The camp eventually came alive with the arrival of new and elaborate equipment whose designated purpose: to help them learn bridge building, lent a shiny spectacle of gleaming silver at the outskirts of the camp boundaries, promising work and adventure in the days ahead. Many soldiers felt the restless call to fill specialist ratings while others wished for transfer. A few, happy with the status quo, bided their time, willing to wait and see. Ernie continued to record their daily activities and sometimes the others looked over his shoulder as he wrote, or reminded him of short pieces of information before "lights out."

A constant change in personnel left Ellis with an overabundance of officers, some of whom had just arrived, and others who stayed to acclimate the recent entourage. Lieutenants Weinstein and Schuster headed up Jean's Company, A, with Sgt. Rhoades in the mess hall and Sgt. White in the supply room. Jean and the other recruits quickly learned their way around and buddied up to Sgt. Rhoades, an intent little guy. The soldiers hoped for extra rations now and then, which almost never materialized, unless the guys went on hunting trips or set rabbit and squirrel traps during what little spare time they had.

The men often found solace at the mail window, built into the end of the supply room, their second most frequent stop after the mess hall, when they were off duty. Some homesick boys longed for any news from home, even newspapers, and others felt fully satisfied to receive a pass to Peoria. Jean, torn between the two desires, felt happy for either outcome as they both came, roughly, with the same irregularity, or most often, not at all.

Although Jean dutifully tried to write home once a week when he didn't have a weekend pass, his letters never suggested anything close to his real thoughts. When Jean got letters from his mother, in reply to his, she always told him about his brothers, Tom still working at home, declined by the military due to eyesight poorer than Jean's own, and Larry in Texas giving the military authorities a hard time.

Her latest note made him recall the time his eldest living brother had profanely declined a Latin verb in school: "Shittae, shittia, shitteo," because his mother implied that he had used similar language in his latest rebellion, at his base in Texas, where he ended up peeling potatoes, piles and piles of potatoes.

George was sent to the Pacific front, and didn't write much, either due to being busy, or because he didn't want to alarm his mother. With the heat in the Tropics, sleep became a welcome relief that spared little time for writing anyway. Norb, now in the European theatre, had taught flight school and become a pilot himself, delivering food and supplies to troops behind the lines in many harrowing missions. At the age of 24, Norb had a crew for which he was responsible, and even though he later reported after the war that his B52 didn't have a square inch not shot up by enemy planes, he only lost one soldier, the gunner, to an injury. He didn't write much either.

On the whole, morale was high in Jean's unit as winter gear, delivered shortly after the bridge building equipment came, buoyed the spirits of everyone who braved the Midwestern winter cold. The heavily lined white fleece parkas served not only to bolster their bodies from the harsh winds, but also as camouflage in the snow. With the hooded coats, Jean and the others received waterproofed boots, the regulation gabardine pants, wooly mittens, heavy jackets for the fields, and thick sleeping bags. It might as well have been Christmas in February with all the rattle of unpackaging, and the scents of new clothing.

All felt ready for their first important training program set to begin at Starved Rock State Park near La Salle for February 8, when, early on the bitterly cold morning the soldiers rose to fires gone out, and they emptied the barracks to stand in formation for the trip, buckled down with their heavy garb and full field packs, bags and rifles, looking like Ernie's written picture of "molded snow men, almost unable to move, as they boarded trucks for the ride through Peoria en route to Starved Rock," the park with the magnificent bluffs overlooking the river.

After stopping for lunch and eating up the rest of the sandwiches packed at breakfast, Jean and the rest of the soldiers re-boarded the trucks and continued to Starved Rock, once an Indian fort with a lookout bluff which allowed a view for miles in the distance. Met by the advance team who showed them to quarters, a series of tarpaper huts once manned by the Civilian Conservation Corp, founded during the Depression by FDR, the men thought these make piece shacks still looked reasonably well considering their former use. How little they knew.

Everyone found a place suitable to their liking, but all soon realized the artic blasts of February air could not be kept from the thin corrugated walls and thin plastic windows, even with the fires built and sleeping bags installed closely together for warmth. After evening chow, the conversations turned more readily to where they might find an evening's entertainment, and many a soldier found their way on weekend passes into different cozy bars in LaSalle filled with the warmth of good beer and camaraderie, Jean included.

Hitting the pillow late one of those nights, Jean lost no time drifting off, fortified as he, and the others were, by alcohol and the elements they had endured all the day long. The woolen blanket bag did little at first to warm his body, but as he sunk into the folds, his last fragmented thoughts before falling into a deep slumber involved the faces of those he loved and missed. Jean's dreams took him to the banks of the flowing Rock River near his home in Rock Island.

The sun sparkled like diamonds on the glassy river near where he and Olie Johnson sat on an embankment created from dried black silt dirt, baiting their fishing rods with fat, wiggling earthworms, dew worms, they called them. Olie taunted Jean that he'd surely be the one to catch the first fish, and they shook hands over a nickel Jean had just minutes before discovered in the mud, both already plotting where to throw their now baited hooks.

The sun-drenched afternoon passed lazily with the smells of the river, the wet earth, the long calls of the birds overhead, and the fish taking them to that quiet place where nature influences mood to the point of meditation. They grazed the deep waters slowly, casting close to the rushing waves near the dam where silver streaks glinted in the bright light. After a time, the silence soothed them, the water sounds rustling into the background.

"Got one!" Olie called suddenly, standing up to better grasp the pole. He wrestled with the tug on his line, reeling in the catch as waves splashed the scrambling fish into the air, fighting for its life. Jean stood too, dropping his own pole in the excitement.

"It's a biggun," he cried, and whopped Olie on the back for support.

Olie expertly wove the fish through watery obstacles, bubbling white caps, and teased its majestic gymnastics to the bank where he pulled the shining creature up to view its full height. Cold fish eyes glared at them ominously.

"I won the nickel," Olie said needlessly, and the two boys exulted in the glory of a summer day on the verge of a much anticipated supper. Both admired the switching fish, unhooked it, and threw it in their bucket of water, knowing they still had the thumping, filleting, and cleaning to do later.

Soon enough, three little fishies and a medium sized catfish joined the big one, and the boys decided to call it an afternoon. Packing up their things, they stood looking into the slowly setting sun, ablaze in oranges and muted reds. Peering out over the waters with their palms covering their eyes, they turned to each other and Jean bragged that he had caught the most. Olie said he had got the biggest. They both grinned. It had been a good day. Now they had presents for their moms.

Across the span of the river, a large black wrought iron bridge stood silhouetted, shining against the sky, a picture of perfection. As in the way of dreams, it shimmered and crystal beads of water on its surface made the structure seem to sway, a hazy light in early evening creating mirages in their minds.

"See that bridge, Olie? One day, I'm going to help build one of those," Jean said. Olie nodded, catching up the bucket of fish with one hand after throwing his pole over his shoulder. He didn't doubt it a bit. Jean had proven his dreams could become reality many times.

By the time military morning arrived, way before actual dawn, Jean felt the warmth of that long ago summer's day in the woolen blanket wrapped around his body, nestled deep inside his sleeping bag, when the bugle call first sounded. Most of the other soldiers felt they, too, had not slept nearly long enough to prepare them for the work ahead.

The A company, divided into platoons, would today sort out the immense task for the upcoming week of building and then tearing down a 20 ton bridge spanning the Rock River. This learning exercise in the chill winds of that February week would test their mettle, and prove their qualifications for being part of the 371st as compared to the other companies, and their efforts to build and tear down the same structures. Jean liked these sorts of tests better than the academic ones.

Later that evening, Ernie would scribble, "In order to manage the final task, they had first had to build a ten ton raft, an infantry support raft bridge, a 20 ton landing raft, a ten ton pontoon bridge, and finally, the famed 20 ton bridge complete with a steel landing barge. All this had to be done in the frigid blasts of February air, on slippery ground and in icy water, on location above the Rock River, regardless of sleet or snow conditions." In other words, in the bitter cold.

Bits of his fishing dream came floating back to Jean as he slicked down his unruly hair and brushed his teeth. He remembered he'd said he'd build a bridge, probably more than one. He remembered watching his brother's crew build the Centennial. He marveled over the memory of watching his mother climb into a car and disappear over the bridge into another state, the state of Iowa. He knew that the fact that his father was a carpenter, and he had mechanical leanings himself had landed him in this unit. He felt lucky to be a part of something big.

Jean and the others dressed quickly to make it to roll call in record time. Once through that, they could hightail it for the mess hall and warm up their insides with hot coffee and hopefully some scrambled eggs. Jean also secretly hoped for a little meat with the rations as he pulled on his boots, folding his socks back into the thick lining, pushing his toes down as far as they would go into the fleece.

The bugler sounded his warning blasts for roll call in the frosty morning air. The band then played a nostalgic version of "Whistle While You Work" as musicians put their mouths to frozen instruments to inspire the soldiers with humor and zeal. The name calling seemed, as usual, to take an endless amount of time, as they waited, stomachs growling. Jean and the others stomped their feet from time to time, stalling the numbness. Red made his usual humorous observations about hurrying up and waiting, while Ernie jotted down other bits of humor in his notebook.

After a hasty meal of thick, hot oatmeal and muddy coffee, with no eggs or meat, the men fell into ranks and marched to the bridge staging area, many thinking ahead to another lazy evening in LaSalle as their hard day's work on various small problems, all preliminaries to the ultimate gargantuan bridge, finally came to an end in the freezing weather. The band played for them when they returned to Ellis for late chow and made their plans for the night's entertainment. Several would play cards, darts, or dice, and some seduce the ladies with conversation or dancing, while others felt content to merely drink and watch. Jean decided he'd see what turned up.

The Rose Bowl Bar, like the ones back home, served food and drinks and provided a homey atmosphere for all the soldiers to pursue their dream of choice. As the crowd grew nosier and more boisterous, Jean found himself caught up in a game of Euchre, but he did not fail to notice the lovely ladies gliding in and out of the groups of men and boys, serving drinks, delivering sandwiches, or simply tidying up the tables. He spied a dark haired dame with deep brown eyes who held his attention all night, but he never got up the courage to talk with her. Too much competition.

Snow fell through the night and again, as the sun tried to peek over the horizon, the tired men tramped through a white haze of covered landscape to the work zone where they began building the 10 ton bridge in the morning, and took it down in the afternoon, with snow still falling, eventually completing the day's assignment. A few grumbled over the futility of tearing down what they had just built, but Jean reasoned they'd need to know how to do both if they were going where he thought they were going.

The small stoves in the tar paper huts usually kept them from freezing, but those returning late from LaSalle in the tired jeeps had no fires as they burned out quickly with no one to tend them. The cold penetrated everything, ripping through gaps in the windows and doorways, and soldiers saw their breaths go before them everywhere. Exhausted from the day's work, and the drive back, Jean whimsically remembered drawing pictures in the mist from breathing cold air onto windows as a child, while he prepared for an early bedtime.

The old two lot homestead with the garage in the far end of the yard, where he used to help Tom, always made him feel warmer. Jean was about ten and the autumn leaves rustled under their feet as they finished waxing the Touring Car which had replaced the old Model T. Jean and Tom flicked their rags back and forth at each other, sometimes hitting, sometimes missing, as they wiped up the rest of the slick wax from the gleaming exterior of the blue vehicle. It looked good. He could see his face in the shining metal.

All of a sudden, Tom handed him the keys, and Tom got into the passenger side of the newly cleaned car, a big grin spreading across his face. Jean didn't have to wait for a better invitation. He climbed into the vehicle and settled into the driver's side, inserting the key into the ignition, straining to see over the steering wheel excitedly. Tom took hold of his arm.

"Only in the yard," he said somberly, "and not too fast!"

Jean pulled himself up to his full height and began to steer slowly through the swirling autumn leaves, his heart keeping pace with the movements of the tires through the lot. Back and forth he drove, not expertly, but with confidence, and soon he picked up a little speed. Tom reached out to steady the wheel, and Jean brushed him off, but not before Tom cleared their way around an old log meant as a stop for parked cars.

Around and around he went, Tom watching, and Jean the one grinning now. Never had he felt so grown up, so in control, and he loved his brother with all his heart for letting him be who he was, a boy in the driver's seat of a real car.

When the bugle sounded next sunrise, the platoon peevishly went about their morning rituals, some still tired from their trip to LaSalle the evening before. Jean had not gone, but those who had partied seemed rather the worse for wear. The day's drill in a murky mist had them making infantry support rafts and training in how to maneuver the large steel landing barge. The cold metal pierced through their wooly mittens, a signal to them they must be careful always of the slippery conditions.

Large blocks of ice swept in by the river's current threatened to make problems for them building the infantry support bridge the next day. Many a man found his feet sliding in the snow and slush, as they tidied up the camp for the day. The air penetrated everything from their ears to their nostrils to their toes, despite their layered clothing. Already hampered by the mud and cold, the men needed another break.

A branch of the USO in LaSalle sponsored a dance for them that last weekend with sweet homemade pies, frosted cakes, sandwiches piled high, and coffee served up along with good music and even more friendly gals. Jean even mustered up a conversation with one of the young women, but not the one he'd noticed earlier in the week. He praised the hospitality of the city, which had to make do with their rations the same as anywhere else, but seemed happy to give to others too. Jean and the other men thanked the servers profusely, feeling rallied by their friendliness.

Jean's sister Catherine worked for the rationing board back home in Rock Island so he knew all too well the stories of shortages in sugar, butter, flour, and other baking necessities, not to mention gasoline and oil. Jean had heard his sister mention once that one old tire had enough rubber in it to make four gas masks. Many were doing without so that the Army had what it needed. The idea of where all this training might put him and his unit made Jean and the others more aware of the people they prepared to protect.

The big day finally arrived when the 20 ton bridge would become reality. By far the most difficult of all their lessons, the soldiers soon knew they would not be finishing early. Icy conditions and having to carry heavy equipment made the men work all the harder to allow them some down time later. Building the balk for the spans between barges nearly broke their backs as everyone trudged in long circles from the tidy piles of wood to the river banks where many of the crew struggled knee deep in waters so cold they turned extremities numb if they did not rotate places often.

Once, carrying heavy equipment to the base of the bridge near the water's edge, Jean felt his feet scrabbling against the slick embankment. As he tried to gain purchase, thoughts of the artic river helped him take hold of himself and maintain his elusive balance, but not before he dropped part of his load and fell onto his hands, wetting his mittens. Trying to prevent the ever-present ice from forming on the wool, Jean took the mitts off and slapped them hard against the equipment. Hands bare, he dug into his pocket and found his lucky coin, the silk of its edge giving him a moment of security, calming him until he caught his breath, exhaling evenly. Before putting his mitts back on, he touched the St. Christopher medal, warm against his chest.

Seeing the barges slide into their places caused joy in the men, and when they at last turned the final screws tightly, not one among them missed the enormity of what they had accomplished as a team. Grumble they might, but the soldiers felt proud of their work and after officers took pictures and inspected the construction, they took down that mighty edifice they had made, and limped home, aching in body, some having fallen in the river for their efforts, almost immediately turned into icicles, but all of them tired and happy, although chilled to the marrow of their bones.

Though they had not broken records in building their bridge, the men had completed their work in less time than the previous crew, and considering the weather, they thought they had managed rather well. Brass seemed to think so because almost everyone planned a final party in LaSalle either with ladies they had already met, or women they hoped to meet. Jean didn't get so lucky, and he never saw the brown-eyed beauty again. Other men like Red, said some ladies promised to write, and some soldiers did get letters, scented with lavender or rose oil. Not many shared those notes.

After these milestones, Company A packed up their belongings, trekked to load up the trucks, and returned to Camp Ellis the next day, reminiscing about their beautiful bridge and the famous ladies of LaSalle. Jean heard stories on the trip back that he surmised might be true, but others, well, Yank said, they just had to be exaggerating.

"You know, though," Yank commented, "Red was gone for a long time before we started back."

Jean nodded. "Probably drank too much, and got lost," he said.

Jack slapped his knee, chortling, as he saw Red sliding over closer.

"If anyone did, it was probably Red," Mikey said.

"What? Get drunk, get lost, or get laid?" Ernie asked.

"I represent those remarks," Red quipped. Red sparked the fire in all the group, instigated food fights, bragged the most, and whined loudly. Still everyone liked him. He always made them laugh. They all secretly hoped he had stolen a few kisses.

The soldiers did not miss the CCC tar paper huts and sub zero temps they left behind on the Rock River, and felt they had dismissed too easily the warmth of their barracks in Ellis, when, stiff and miserable, they fell into these bunks back near Macomb, leaving their exercise in bridge building, the beautiful wrought iron icy maiden, behind, but not forgotten, as memories of the bridge construction faded into their prayers and restless dreams.

CHAPTER 3

Mechanical Leanings

On the way back from Starved Rock, one of the men in the company tried to disappear into the trees, but after roll call in the trucks, the officers finally figured out which soldier was gone, and dispatched several to look for him. Alone, without food, and only a little water, the stray eventually got captured, and the others, already back at Ellis, witnessed him, retrieved, manacled, and surly, being marched to the brig, where, after further investigation, he received a section 8 discharge.

Company A, sobered by this quiet but stirring spectacle, mused over what would become of the fugitive in his distant future, marked by a dishonorable discharge, and more importantly, what would become of Company A? Mikey mumbled that he wouldn't want to be in that man's shoes. A few of the other men murmured their own misgivings, but Jean pondered the last time he had seen a man shackled.

Back in Catholic grade school, located across the street from the court house, he and the other boys gathered at the window, to watch a scheduled hanging, as the girls dutifully followed Sister Mary Vincent to the restroom. They had all heard for days what was going to happen, and exulted as the timing happened to fall just right, during the girls' bathroom break, when the boys remained unsupervised.

They watched the prisoner led out to the platform where a crowd had gathered. Bound tightly, stumbling toward the shadowy rope hanging high above his head, the convicted man looked up and saw his fate before him. Jean and the others buzzed with overt, frightened excitement, and carried their noisy exclamations through the open window over the breeze to where, Jean was sure, the man looked across, straight at him.

A policeman swooped the rope over the criminal's neck and the crowd grew quiet. The boys followed suit, so intent they did not notice Sister coming back into the room, wondering if the boys' silence meant they were up to something. Seeing them gathered at the window, Sister's memory kicked into gear, and she shooed the observant group away from the sight they were not meant to see, corralling them into the corner to line up for their own trip to the toilets, as the girls trailed into the room.

Now, all grown up, Jean shivered at the memory as Company A prepared to listen to more lectures in the academic setting Jean detested, their bunks pushed back and used as seats for the classes. Ernie took notes and later wrote, "They studied Malaria Control, First Aid, Map Reading, Tent Pitching, and The Care and Use of Fire Arms once again. Officers of each company, and later, some of the sergeants and even corporals taught the classes, rotating from barracks to barracks, platoon to platoon." Short breaks allowed the men time to wrestle, write a short letter, use the restroom, or to go right on sleeping.

The morning program always started with marching as a morale builder to the "Whistle While You Work" ditty they had all become accustomed to hearing, even in their sleep. Slow footed men learned to shuffle off to a left turn, then a right, and, at a moment's notice, "Forward March," the command they all dreaded to hear as they watched steam rise from their nostrils in the early morning air. "Cooks in their soiled whites added color to the lines as the soldiers hardly stopped to salute the colonel in the dim light of the predawn drills, struggling to keep up with the others," Ernie later recorded the maneuvers, step by step, reading his clear observations to the others before they hauled themselves off to bed.

Collars up, rifles on shoulders, helmets pulled over knitted hoods, the soldiers sometimes did whistle, and other times they snorted with laughter during the nonconformist lip and tongue noises uttered while they did their "Walk Around." Those who couldn't whistle preferred their own musical notes. Someone, usually led by Red, had a snippet of decadence to deliver under his breath to break up the long drill. Even shy Mikey added surprising sounds to the mix, encouraged by the other remarks.

Months of practice had them all moving without thinking, and sometimes, stray soldiers slipped unnoticed into the already formed ranks after catching a few extra winks, or having a leisurely bowel movement. If anyone saw, no one commented, and the monotonous tedium continued day after day, stretching into weeks as they marched mornings, ate a hasty lunch, then broke down to go back to the barracks for long afternoon academics once again.

Ernie had a crowd around him that night as he read about the afternoon's schooling. "Motion pictures on security training signaled by screeching bugles found the men mouthing bits of conversations to each other before the images on the screens began to speak as they had seen most of the films more than once. As bits about Nazi agents and submarines stalking wound down into spinning reels, yet another movie about mosquitoes, or Why We Fight, appeared on the horizon of learning. Originally eight films scheduled to build morale ended abruptly after the fifth installment. The other three had mysteriously disappeared and no one ever told how or why, but all whispered stories, and Ernie's written accounts hinted where."

Eventually, their heads crammed with all variety of lessons, their feet sore from marching, the men heard rumors about upcoming railroad details. Since many would probably have to work on these, as well as bridges, overseas, two groups would be sent out, one to Bradford, and one to Bloomington to work on laying the tracks and explore life living in rail cars, learning real skills about laying track from real railroad men, and working regular hours like civilians. The men heard they would have plenty of free time to explore the cities where they worked of an evening, and that provided incentive to go.

As gossip about the new orders permeated the camp, Jean spent any free time he got down by the motor pool, helping out on the care and maintenance of their loaned Army vehicles, volunteering to do regular upkeep on the jeeps. He knew that job firsthand, thanks to Tom.

He remembered first working for Irish Cab owned by his cousins, Basil and Barney, in Rock Island when he was a young teen. They let him run the desk and dole out the keys to the employees as they checked in for work. Gradually he began to take calls and dispatch addresses to the drivers who called in on their walkie-talkies. In his down time, he washed and waxed the cabs not in use, and eventually began to change the oil and spark plugs in all the vehicles on a regular basis.

Basil, otherwise known as Irish, finally let him drive one day when one of the employees called in sick. After that, Jean picked up calls whenever and wherever he could, and still manned the desk as needed. He adapted to the life readily, and became a regular cabbie as soon as he got home from school, changed his clothes, and snatched a bite to eat. On weekends, he spent most of the day in the cab bay, or on the road, finding streets he never knew existed, learning to deal with rude customers, and making exact change.

Basil found he could depend on Jean, and Jean loved the feeling of getting paid a small salary for doing something he loved to do. He even drove the taxi to Mass on Sundays, and once, when he found no other place to park, he maneuvered the car into a space right in front of the church. When Monsignor came into the altar area, he stepped up to the podium and all but shouted, "Whoever parked that damn taxi in front of God's house, move it immediately!"

Never had Jean been so glad to have sat in the back of the church, as he quietly got up, collected his cap, and made for the door, the congregation quiet, save for a few snickers, but their necks craning to see who had shown such audacity. Neck flaming with heat, Jean decided not to ever go back to Mass in the taxi, and especially not to Monsignor's church.

When orders for departure to work on the rails came, Jean wasn't among the groups bound for the railroads. A little disappointed, he meandered down to the motor pool and sat on one of the turned over barrels to see what was going on. The news about who was coming and going, and where, always started there.

Jean knew he could get a trip to the post office in the next city to pick up mail, if nothing else.

His aptitude for fixing cars did not go unnoticed, as many times, between marching and lectures, he received instructions to report to the motor pool to work on oil changes, spark plugs, or faulty ignition switches. When nothing else could be done, he washed the jeeps, and painstakingly wiped down the tires, always caked with mud. He felt at home among the jeeps and the smells of oil and gas. Here, Jean also heard the new orders for those not sent to work on the railroad in Bradford.

The 86 members of Company A left behind, together with the stragglers from the other companies would go to Shawnee National Forest in southern Illinois for maneuvers. Playing war as adults did not have the pleasure it had held for them as boys when they had complete control of their game, because the Army made the adult version as tough as possible. The 240 mile trip by truck to their battlefield began the last day of February in the bitter cold.

The soldiers dug foxholes and broke into two assigned teams, the red and the blue, both supposedly wanting possession of the same land. Huddling in groups with "their rifles loaded with blank rounds and firecrackers for hand grenades, the thrill of battle began with each of them feeling almost like a veteran already," Ernie later noted in his chronicles. Company A's reds took the advantage at first by pushing the blues back, but the next day, after a hasty supper around small camps in the freezing temperatures, the blues seemingly disappeared, making the reds scout the area, until, finding their opponents, rested and waiting, the reds had their own experience of retreating.

Finally on March 5, in the winter rain, the blues bombarded the defensive positions the reds prepared, pushing them even further back, and finally attacking and conquering them in a battle that went on until well into the night. Feeling well-worn and cold to the core, the men got orders to pack up the next day after hearing the report of casualties (prisoners taken), and injuries, the worst among them "a massive black eye caused by the butt end of a rifle, and a two-fisted brawl before the resulting capture," as reported by Ernie.

Many stories about the brawl and their own escapades during the war game passed from group to group as they compared their own prowess against the accounts of others. Bravado and exaggeration trumped reality as their fantasies of glory and patriotism turned cold in the wake of these chilling bouts of make believe battles, which warned them what was coming.

The whole experience of playing war wearied them immensely, giving them no time to do anything but eat and sleep in snatches during the stretches of time when they were not pursuing or pursued, or planning their maneuvers. The trenches, when they had actually slept in them, were warmer than level ground, but not much, and the canned rations did little to fill their stomachs. Jean noted that the rumbling in his own stomach stemmed from more than lack of food.

Encamped between skirmishes, talk had scrambled around how close to being real their game might be. No one's thoughts escaped the fact that this exercise in mere child's play would probably be nothing like the actual battlefields on their horizons.

"You think we'll have to sleep outside like this over there?" Mikey asked from the dark, the whites of his eyes just visible in the sparse moonlight.

"We won't have featherbeds, I'm sure," Jean replied. The others chuckled softly, careful not to make too much noise.

"No hotels, either," Jack mumbled.

"Do ya think Hitler cares his own men sleep in trenches?" Red asked sarcastically.

"That bastard? Hell, no," Yank said, his breath spiraling around the spoken words as he exhaled them.

"Hitler doesn't care about anything except power," Ernie said quietly.

The others had grunted their approval of Ernie's assessment. Snippets of conversations like this came back to Jean as they packed up their gear and cleaned up the grounds as best they could before the trip back. Jean remembered watching a war movie as a boy that had enthralled him.

"Anyone ever see All Quiet on the Western Front?" he asked, while stowing his belongings.

"Yes, with Lew Ayers. Did you read the book?" Ernie asked, as he tossed some tin cans into a garbage sack.

"No, I didn't." Jean said.

"Book was better." Ernie returned.

"I wasn't old enough to read then," Jean said with a grin.

"Me neither," Jack chimed in.

"What was it about?" Mikey asked, throwing his duffel bag over his shoulder.

"WWI," Jean replied, taking time to pause before loading his bag onto his shoulder.

"Written by a German soldier, Erich Maria Remarque." Ernie added.

"Ah, wasn't that the bloke who came to America and hangs out in Hollywood?" Red asked.

"Yes," Ernie answered. "Germany is already banning and burning his books. He had to get out."

"Did it make a difference in the story that a German soldier wrote it?" Mikey asked.

"Apparently, the Germans thought so because they're banning and burning it," Yank said.

"No, that's what's weird. He could have been any one of us," Ernie replied. "I guess you're right though, Yank. The Germans didn't like it, and that's why we're back over here, fighting their world view," Ernie nodded to Jean, "What parts do you remember?"

"The part I remember most is the soldiers under fire taking cover in a graveyard, hiding under the dead bodies," Jean said.

"I remember the convoy of coffins arriving after that battle," Ernie said, "and of course, the final scene, which was a complete shock."

Jean felt a shiver go up his spine, recalling the totally unexpected ending.

"Aren't you glad you asked, Mikey?" Yank pulled his gear up to his shoulder. Mikey shook his head no. Everyone was strangely quiet after that.

Again, the men welcomed their return to Ellis, their three warm stoves, and double decker bunks with actual blankets. Even the mess hall food seemed gourmet after a week in the forest depending on canned rations. All told their individual stories and joked over the war charade, but each one, alone with his thoughts before bed, knew that soon, the real game, with real bullets, could commence, and that thought haunted their dreams.

After a day or two back in camp, the men who had been playing war games traded training exercises with the railroad workers becoming soldiers maneuvering in the forest, and the reds and blues learning the world of rails from men who worked them daily and had time to prowl nearby cities until late night. So life continued until all soldiers returned to Ellis and a new round of lectures and training started with the endless marching, and the boring lessons. This time around, an added air of cleanup sparked the men's attention to detail.

New physicals, vaccinations, dental exams, vision checks, haircuts, inspections, and clothing and equipment upgrades made the soldiers sense their home soil eroding beneath their feet. Last minute checklists of men who missed this training or that lecture due to illness brought slackers up to speed. Every soldier had to take refresher courses on shooting, sniper training, and hand to hand combat. Jean earned his sniper certification, too, in spite of his one eye being below normal vision limits.

A scramble for passes and furlough trains boarding to Chicago and St. Louis, and Sundays spent with families meant little time left for goodbyes and for saying things left unsaid. Visits to neighboring areas of the camp increased as wives, girlfriends, and family members came to say their goodbyes. Jean noted that he saw more long, drawn-out kisses than he'd ever seen in the movies. A kind of mass confusion existed in the barracks and in their minds.

At home for his last furlough in Rock Island, his family wanted Jean to wear his uniform, but he refused, saying he lived in it too much already. Awkward silences spread as cousins and other relatives wished him well before his departure, and Jean felt glad to have his mother's home cooking satisfy his appetite before leaving home yet again.

Those last rainy days at Ellis brought another appeal from area farmers as the soldiers helped them build walls against the flooding rivers, making barricades with sand and logs.

By April, the barrage of water falling made mud of their own camp, with jeeps and trucks getting stuck so that orders came to lay sod, "scalped from pastures in the countryside and positioned in mud as endless as the spring rains," according to

Ernie's chronicle, all in addition to their daily routines. Ernie scribbled that even "cats" got stuck, men slid into mud almost calf deep, and "forty acres of land showed a ruined swirl of knee deep ruts where cows once grazed."

For entertainment after this backbreaking landscaping, the camp enjoyed watching the Air Force demonstrate its aerial skills as pilots simulated an air attack on dummy tanks while all of Ellis' personnel sat on high bluffs near Spoon River, able to take in the majesty of the spectacle below from a place beneath the skies but far above the earth. Everyone felt the march there and back more than worth their while, as the sun rose on a pretty day and the fresh spring air invigorated their lungs. All slept well that night.

Still, as days wound down, anxiety built, and although the last passes required everyone to be back in camp by 5:30 Sunday morning, many men swore they'd be AWOL their last day. Though many did not return on time, no one, not even the brass mentioned it. That Monday, final instructions given included the fact that each soldier had to fit all his belongings into one duffel bag, resulting in many over-packed canvases with buckles bulging.

On May 3rd they boarded the long train that took them on their journey east, a slow journey, interspersed with quiet stories, eating and sleeping, low keyed card games, and some reading or writing. Traveling through the Windy City of Chicago's, skyscrapers, to Ohio and on to Pennsylvania and New York, and finally Boston, the men got to know each other even better, and made a mess of their railway cars. What laughter rang through the train surprised the other men, and thus began their total blackout of their American homeland.

CHAPTER 4

An Ocean Voyage

The 371st Engineers got their orders to depart for Europe and a whole new outlook consumed the men. This was it. They were going to the show. The hustle and bustle of preparing to travel made for excitement, and anticipation, but also a healthy dread, the primary mood of the company. All talk centered around the next stage of their lives, and of the journey they all knew they must make to another world, the world of war. With fresh haircuts they made their last censored calls, and prepared for the trip over the pond.

Jean, having grown up on the mighty Mississippi, didn't feel the call of the Atlantic the way some of the other men did. He had never even learned to swim properly, and truth be told, the wide expanse of the ocean frightened him. Still, the fresh, salty smell of the waters, miles from the shore, captivated them, Jean included. As they neared the edge of the continent, the white capped green waves beckoned them to distant horizons seen as a complement to the blue skies against the backdrop of the glinting sun. No one could deny the beauty of the scene. Jean realized he could even smell the water, a fresh sea salt scent.

Under the scrutinizing eyes of the FBI and the military police on May 10th the men began loading their belongings and the heavy equipment they would need "over there" onto a huge ship in the Boston harbor, called the SS Brazil, which gleamed, silver-grey, next to the bright waters, almost emerald in color. Unfamiliar sights and sounds, and the compelling smell of the briny sea, braced the men for their first walk on the wavering floor of the plank shaking them onto their passage to their new seafaring quarters, deep in the bowels of the biggest ship they had ever seen.

"Wow, would you look at these barracks!" Yank intoned deeply, as they descended into the quarters of the great vessel, inspecting the ship's offerings. Crammed together in long rows, the iron beds, stacked three deep, sparse as they seemed, still managed to look a step up from the barracks they had left. Each one had crisp, clean sheets and a woolen blanket roll. Pushing and shoving their way to the interior, each man made choices about which bunk and which bunk mates might best facilitate their long crossing. Jean, Mikey, and Red, grabbed empty beds across from Yank, Jack and Ernie.

"No passing gas in these close quarters," Red announced as he inspected the small beds.

"Says the master of the art," Mikey drawled.

"Hey, we've all been guilty of that," Jack observed as he patted a flat pillow into a roll.

"We're gonna have to make sure we're not under any bed wetters," Yank noted.

"Oh, Lord," Ernie shook his head. "You would have to remind us of that." He sat down suddenly with a plop as the ship lurched slightly.

"Anyone else's stomach rolling?" Jean asked.

Already many of the men felt the overpowering nausea of the rocking ship threaten to embarrass them in front of their companions. Jean felt the sway of the water under the still anchored ship change from gently swishing, frothy caps to relentless washes of waves bombarding the boat as he, too, sat and watched other soldiers stash their belongings in small duffel sized spaces between the beds, and claim their spaces, readying for the launch of their long voyage.

On May 13th when finally, the boat's whistle blew, the huge ship sauntered slowly into the deep Atlantic, parting the churning waves as it moved forward, inching away from their homeland and taking them to the world from which their ancestors came.

Late that night, after a small supper of sandwiches, one of only two meals a day, had somewhat sated their appetites, and those assigned kitchen duty properly stowed and straightened in the kitchen, the men wandered onto the decks, smoked, or settled into the hard metal beds, calling out their good nights and joking about their comrades still in the commode, or on deck, lunging over the railing, retching their dinner into the vast waters. Many of them had spent some time in those places already.

Jean plumped his small pillow and turned onto his side, facing the wall. Sleep would not come despite the rocking of the ship. His thoughts tangled, Jean again remembered home, as he often did before bed. Trying to say some prayers, he drifted in and out of that first sleep state, hearing new noises and absorbing old reminders of sleeping with a crowd, the low grunts and creaking beds as soldiers tried to get comfortable in the cramped spaces. The roar of conversations and settling in deepened to a quiet hum. Jean heard snores of those already claimed by dreams and the white noise lulled him to close his eyes.

The ship slipped into an icy chill and dusk drove the background of the dreamscape into darkness. Out from that hazy mist emerged the figure of an older but familiar woman garbed in frothy white, much like the waves of the ocean at twilight. She glided toward him, three feet above the floor, moving closer and then stopping. No sound came from her lips, but Jean recognized his grandmother Mag.

As in the way with dreams, her mouth moved over and over, and she seemed to be trying to tell him something important, but Jean could not hear her, or even read her lips. Her gaze was insistent, her gestures urgent. Then, as if exasperated because he could not understand her message, Mag's hand reached out from under her flowing shawl, touched him, and woke him with icy coldness, startling him, spiraling him into the wakeful dread of the unknown.

"Hey, how did you sleep?" Yank in the bunk across from him asked, as they hurried to answer the call of the bugle announcing the day's beginning. He seemed concerned.

"Not so well," Jean mumbled, remembering the strange dream, his grandmother's frigid, marbled touch, and the distant sense that he had somehow missed her message.

"Thought so," his new friend acknowledged. "You were talking in your sleep."

"What did I say?" Jean asked, worried.

"Nothing I could understand," the soldier said, pulling his shirt over his head.

"Strange dream," Jean mumbled.

Throughout the day Jean pondered the meaning of his night's reverie and wondered at the timing of such a visit from his mother's mother. His family often seemed to have mystical leanings. He vividly remembered the stories of his youth about the gold buried in the bathroom as he dressed for roll call. Feeling the rumbling in his stomach, he headed to the deck, musing quietly, lost in thought, pulling on his shoe laces as he climbed the ladder to a predawn light.

During the Depression his grandfather had not trusted banks with his coins. The family knew he had buried a considerable sum, but unfortunately, not until after grandpa's death did they think to wonder or ask where. Much time and discussion passed as the old man's stash disappeared further from discovery more each day. Long after conversations suggesting possible hiding places dwindled to almost no memory of the loss, Jean's mother had a strange dream herself.

Standing in the bright early morning light, waiting for the count, and the call of his name, Jean ruminated on the story he had heard several times.

Asleep in her rocker, Maryanne felt the presence of a woman in white, hovering near. Again, as in the way of dreams, no words passed, but the angelic white-clad lady communicated that the gold rested somewhere under the bathroom floor of the house Maryanne's husband's father had built, the house they now lived in. When she woke, wondering at the strangeness of her dream, Maryanne told the story to each of her sons as they wandered in from school or work, and the boys excitedly decided to dig up the wood and dirt flooring.

After turning up most of the dirt beneath the bathroom floor, arguing over whose turn it was to shovel next, and making a huge mess, the boys heard their father come in. Despairing of finding anything, but not wanting their dad to think them fools, they hastened to tell the story of their mother's dream, everyone chiming in at once. Maryanne, wiping the flour on her hands onto the bulky apron at her waist, then repeated the tale in calmer fashion to her bewildered husband.

Fred lifted the shovel then, and set to work, intrigued by the notion. The boys watched in amazement as the metal of the shovel suddenly struck something hard, making a tinkling sound. Fred bent, and carefully removing the dirt around the object, revealed a glass canning jar wrapped in canvas filled with sunny coin, clinking against the glass as Fred raised it to the light. The contents eventually yielded $495, counted many times by each of the boys under the watchful eyes of their dad, a small fortune during the Depression. Later, Fred, after cleaning his hands, and staring at the gleaming stacked coins, declared he would take the money to his mother right after dinner.

"But I haven't got the dinner ready," Maryanne wailed. "I've been too busy running back and forth from kitchen to bathroom."

That one night, no one cared dinner was late.

Jean could almost hear his mother's far-away voice as he sat down to his own breakfast on the ship of thick cream of wheat with lumps in it. Amidst the noise, he withdrew into that other time, remembering the rest of the story.

The males decided to take a quick walk across the street to their father's mother's home, also built by their grandfather. Fred scooped the money back into the dirty jar and left Maryanne to the stove and their simmering supper.

Overwhelmed at someone having found the lost gold at last, Fred's mother counted out $100 and slid it clumsily into her son's direction. His eyes grew as wide as the coins in instant protest, as he juggled the weight of his recent discovery in his now open palms.

"It's yours, Ma," he stated adamantly.

"No, your father would say you earned it," she replied firmly. The rest she kept, and distributed as needed, to other family members throughout those lean years.

His own family had often discussed the ways and means of the dream coming when it did, during the Great Depression, and the manner in which the message appeared. No one, however, doubted the very real response to the prompt from the figure in white roaming the ceiling of Maryanne's mind. Whether real or a dream, the unknown woman gave them a message. The money had materialized, exactly at the time they needed it most.

Jean roused himself from his mental wanderings and tried to bring himself back to the everyday requirements of being on ship with his company headed for Europe. As when he had been in school, those in authority noted his daydreaming and a few marked it as laziness, but Jean knew that the subconscious speaks, and he measured the wordless communication he had received, in the late night as he had slept, against the unknown scenario looming before him.

In the convoy, a city of some 100 ships, in transport to an unknown destination, the men spent time watching movies, having boxing matches, playing craps or poker, (and some even made wagers they later regretted), making airplanes, and even flying kites after they completed their day's chores which consisted of KP duty for most, and endless inspections and refresher courses for others. Then the groups rotated.

Jean spent any free time he had watching the ocean from the ship's rail. He started by looking at the wide, deep expanse of water stretching out to the horizons all around. In the dark, under the stars, Jean remembered a quotation Sister Annelle used to put on the blackboard every year, and since he had her a couple or three times, due to not passing math, and he really liked the quotation, he remembered it.

"You cannot throw a pebble into the water without its ripples reaching all the stars."

Taking in the vast surroundings under the moon and stars, Jean sighed with satisfaction as he realized just how very close to the stars the water seemed to rest, then churn, and eventually, sometimes, roll into the sky and touch the twinkling lights. The universe proved wonders existed every day, and the level of meanings in that simple, chalked statement of Sister Annelle's reminded him of the consequences of every action causing worlds of results.

Then, he turned to the depths of the ocean, looking down into the waters where waves and waves of liquid green splashed against the sides of the ship and as far down as he could see into the darkness. He wondered how far into the darkness the water went, and shivered a little, thinking about how he couldn't swim. He had always wondered what he'd do if he ever fell into water over his head while fishing.

On stormy nights, sometimes alone, and sometimes with his buddies, Jean helped secure all the loose objects on deck, and afterwards, wandered to the edge of their home on water, marveling at the power engulfing them. Finding places to stand outside the elements and under easements gave them a chance to voice their wonder.

"Will you look at that water dancing on the wind?" Jean hollered over the noise.

"It's beautiful," Ernie called back.

"Scares me to death," Mikey shivered as a wave jumped up and almost grabbed him.

"We'll hafta be wearing life jackets on board the deck if this keeps up," Yank observed.

"Either that, or go below deck like normal people," Red said drily.

"Who's got a cigarette," Mikey asked.

"Don't you mean who's got a lighter that will withstand the spray?" Ernie chuckled.

Yank checked his pocket, and pulled out both, handing them over to Mikey who stepped as far back against the wall as he could get. He and Yank, and then Red, passed around the cigarette, leaving Ernie, Jack and Jean to reflect more on the storm.

"These waters aren't safe," Ernie said.

"Who knows how far the Germans send ships this way?" Jack asked.

"No kidding," Jean replied, thinking of their destination and the possibility of German subs patrolling off the coast of England, and possibly closer to them than they thought.

"We'll soon be in the center of it all. The European Theatre," Ernie shook his head as a huge gust of water splattered his face.

"The perfect storm," Jean said, "Good vs. evil."

"The perfect plot," Jack said, turning to avoid a huge wave, and to see the cigarettes under the eaves sputtering out in the fingers of their friends from the powerful splash.

While these daily responsibilities, diversions, and little pleasures helped the time go faster, the crossing seemed to take forever, and indeed, it wasn't until May 21st that some of the men called to the others that they could dimly distinguish the outlines of land they thought to be Ireland. After eleven days at sea, getting to know one another, sometimes too well in close quarters, most of the soldiers seemed relieved to see the shores of England, their planned destination, soon take shape.

Jean and his buddies had come to feel a bond like family, as, when on the train, their free time on the ship, without drills and marching, allowed them to reveal more and more of their individual quirks, sometimes funny, sometimes annoying.

Red, for example revealed that his humorous disposition compensated for his unfunny life as an orphan, "Tumbling up, as Charles Dickens so aptly put it, on my own. I'm the American version of an English pickpocket," Red bragged as he began straightening his bed and his belongings.

"You're obviously well educated if you know Dickens," Ernie complimented him.

"'Twas the sisters in the orphanages that gave us an education," Red said. "And if we didn't get it, they rapped us hard on the knuckles." He grinned and drummed his fingers against the bed's iron rail, suddenly splaying his fingers to display a coin he'd confiscated from an unsuspecting pillow, to the amazement of all.

Jean groaned, remembering similar experiences with his own tender knuckles.

Yank told his own tale of hoping to settle down one day with his pretty girlfriend. Sharing a picture of a short blonde with an engaging smile and deep blue eyes, Yank confessed to having given her an engagement ring before he had boarded the train to go east. "She told me if I didn't come back to her, she'd kill me herself." Yank smiled, slipping the well worn picture back into his pocket over his sentimental heart.

"You'll be Mutt and Jeff," Red quipped, noting that Yank towered over 6 feet and his lady looked about 5' 2". Company A had gotten all the tallest soldiers assigned to it.

Ernie, their writer, shared stories of his education and of his dreams to do something wonderful someday. He hoped to use his knowledge to teach or write, and he pulled a crisp photograph out of his slender billfold of his dazzling wife, Charlotte, with wavy, cropped brown hair, and sparkling eyes, dressed in a short skirt that showed off her shapely legs, and their small son squirming in her arms.

Just then everyone teased Mikey for his constant bouts of growling stomach, and the subsequent sounds of discontent that made the rest of them go for cover away from the smells. Returning slowly to their little circle, gathered now on the ship deck with a view behind them like a picture post card, Mikey grinned, and the blush on his face barely showed in the early dawn shadows. "I'm going to buy horses and get rich racing them when we go back," Mikey blurted. "You just wait and see."

"You wish," Red said good-naturedly, clapping his hand over Mikey's shoulder with affection.

"I'll probably be mucking out stalls," Jack said.

"What about you, Jean?" Ernie asked.

Jean hadn't decided. He shrugged his shoulders, lifted his eyebrows, and said, "Maybe a Tom Sawyer enterprising type. Who knows?" He lowered his voice and spoke deeply, elongating the syllables in the last two words.

"The Shadow knows...." Red droned in a deep, foreboding voice, before he cackled in a hideous laugh, bringing back their memories of the old radio show they had all grown up hearing.

As the ship slid into the entrance to Liverpool Harbor, the male testosterone levels jumped off the charts when they saw the fishing skiffs and packed ferries which held pretty English girls with fair skin and dark hair. Making fools of themselves, the guys whistled and waved, and shouted themselves hoarse, only to find they would be anchored and bunked in their ship yet another night. In the dim twilight, just before lights out, much talk about the women they had seen made conversations turn bawdy, and some of the men began to tell their stories of conquests past and to come. The talk and the laughter got loud before things tapered off to quieter discussions. Eventually these became whispered exchanges as the darkness, and their secret desires soon enveloped them, the friction of their blankets masking their fears, even if only for a brief time, as sleep took hold of them, their last night in the SS Brazil.

England

After seeing it from afar, and setting foot on the land, in merry old England, the water-weary soldiers couldn't help but notice the bright colors all around, the tightly constructed factory buildings with rusty old brick in the cities, and soon, the rolling green landscapes on the outskirts of cities, towns and villages with well kept gardens and riots of flowers everywhere. Some of the men began imitating the clipped British accents they heard everywhere, and tipping their hats to the ladies, who, smiling, couldn't help but pay attention to the noisy, boy-like males with boisterous voices and engaging smiles.

The soldiers felt their libidos growing as they watched the women walking, their short skirts showing off their toned, muscled legs, and their shapely ankles in heels clicking against cobblestones, making their behinds do amazing things. A collective sigh seemed to feed off the sensual mood as soldiers whistled under their breaths at the fairer sex who provided them with images of faces and other body parts they'd remember long into many a night.

The city of cobblestone streets also provided plenty to see as they all walked from the boat to the train station carrying their own bags and whatever smaller equipment they could manage in the heat of the morning. The 371st realized that, what few automobiles existed, traveled on the left side of the street, and the noise and bustle of the harbor city began to awaken with the sounds of shopkeepers clamoring for their first customers.

Upon arrival at the train depot, and being met with piping hot doughnuts and steaming coffee served by the Red Cross, just as if the pretty volunteers had stepped from Boston to Liverpool with them, the men sniffed the air appreciatively, fraught with scented cologne, and fresh soap and shampoo, and other female smells as they picked up newspapers and settled in, loading the train until late in the day on the 25th of May, but taking the time to savor their food and other appetites. Being on solid ground also soothed many a soldier's stomach.

Not aware of their actual destination, rumors suggested it would be at least an overnight journey through the wondrous miniature landscaped greenery and cottages laced by elaborate trees and gardens filled with ripening fruits and vegetables to sustain the English during these difficult times, not unlike the victory gardens back home. The fully manicured, compartmentalized train seemed to personify the land itself with tidy, economical, but comfortable cars that each held four men.

Traveling through Manchester, the train conductors reported it would soon be time to black out the windows and sleep. The fast pace of the train lulled Jean to a restless state as he tried to find room for his ever-growing legs in the small space allotted to him, Red, Mikey, and Yank. Ernie and Jack had joined the next group. After everyone got the small talk of the day's activities out of the way, in the dark, Yank ventured to ask the inevitable question.

"Do you think we're heading into the nightmare?"

"Ah, it's only going to be a bad dream," Red spat back. "First, we get to see some sights and meet some girls."

"I hope you're right." Mikey said dubiously.

"About damn time," Yank said, scratching his crotch.

The others laughed.

"Hey, aren't you engaged?" Red taunted.

"Sure am, and ready to practice," Yank said, grinning. Then he touched his pocket, the one where he kept his picture of his fiancée. "Sorry, baby," he murmured.

"We'll probably see more practice building bridges," Mikey mused after the laughter died down.

"We are the 371st Engineers," Jean noted finally, "so we'll be before or after most action."

"Or, maybe in the middle of it," Red observed drily.

The next morning, the train made its way into Salisbury. As the groggy soldiers disembarked, waiting trucks collected them and their belongings for the convoy to Druids Lodge on the plains. Some expected an elegant dwelling, but their dream turned into tents, rows and rows of tents shaped like teepees, stretching over hillsides surrounded by woods for deep cover. Ernie said he had heard an officer mention the place had been a golf course at one time. They set up camp over most of the day and did their usual chores.

The best thing about settling down for the night came in the form of mail bags with more mail than they had seen in at least three weeks, and almost everyone, Jean included, reading letters from loved ones and, once in a while, sharing pictures or tidbits of information from home as the hushed atmosphere in the camp made their surroundings seem like a quiet library, at least for a short time.

One man, a row over laughed out loud, shouting, "My Ma says in her letter to me that some moron wrote the FBI asking why the Shadow couldn't be sent to kill Hitler. Can you believe that?"

Laughter erupted, but a few remembered a previous conversation. Mikey and Yank high fived, and then hand slapped Jean, who reached out to Jack, who nudged Ernie, looking up from his notebook and smiling, before Red intoned in a rich baritone voice, "The Shadow knows…."

"Daylight lasted until well past 2300 hours, showing the change in latitude in England, considerably north of the States," Ernie read what he had just written before bed, "And dawn was also earlier," he finished, sharing with the others.

"Translated, that means England lies north of most of the USA," Red said, and Ernie laughed.

So life in the European Theatre began. Everything hinged on rudimentary details, basic rations out of tin cans, fending more for self, showing and taking the initiative, and of course, another orientation on drill, this time a drill with gas masks, oh, and more lectures. Most importantly, the men realized how close they were to the front when they had to dig their own trenches around the city of tents, just in case the Germans spotted their camp from overhead while looking for places to drop their bombs. Jean remembered the silver coin in his pocket as he paused in the digging, and reached to feel its secure edge through his trousers, and then felt for the medal under his shirt.

The return to such strict routine annoyed the men so much that during their first inspection parade in England, the battalion bit back at the brass. During the commands, given by the now infamous Colonel Adcock, the men commenced to chime in unison with the command being given so that an echo sounded throughout the lines. Nervous officers, concerned over the minor rebellion, and embarrassed by the impression they made on the English bystanders, began to look for instigators among the ranks, like teachers in a classroom scanning the room for class clowns, as the ceremony continued, uninterrupted, but fraught with subdued snickers.

At ease after the demonstration, the men noticed a meeting of the high mucky mucks, as the soldiers marched back to their tented city, and the low hum of incessant chatter among the men caused the officers to halt the line and demand the perpetrators to turn themselves in. "Silence prevailed, except for a few uncomfortable coughs, but the troops paid for their mockery with extra drills in the late evening, and later, the officers dreamed up a punishment no one liked, the Honey Detail, also deemed the psychology experiment," Ernie read later.

All the privates, Jean and his friends included, except for Ernie, who was first class, got latrine duty, taking command of cleaning the three latrines in the camp. After three or four days of this duty, the officers rotated the teams, and hoped the example of this punishment would improve the rank and file behavior. In fact, it did the opposite, but the privates knew better than to fight back this time.

Using buckets, the detail of four men at a time, two, sometimes three different times a day, had to retrieve the waste of the camp in buckets, which they then carried to outlying areas and burned. Tending these buckets, precariously carrying them, they resembled men caring for bee hives as they danced their way from the latrines to the burning area, trying hard not to get stung, or splattered by the waste they hauled in both hands, noses uncovered.

After getting a second order to the Honey Detail, and noting not one of the other privates that he knew had, Jean went back to his tent and told the others. Razzing him until he felt his temper rise, Jean jerked away from Ernie's gentle hand on his forearm. Ernie told him to take it to Sarge. "See what's what," Ernie told him.

So Jean took his orders to Sarge, whom he found near the motor pool. Jean respectfully saluted and asked permission to speak. Permission granted, Jean looked at the officer sheepishly.

"Sir, why did I get assigned to the Honey Detail again? Sir, nobody else got a second time."

The sergeant removed his cap from his sweaty forehead and wiped his brow with a handkerchief. After looking over his shoulder, and seeing no one in the vicinity, he then leaned forward.

"You really want to know why?" Sergeant asked.

"Sir, yes, sir!" Jean replied.

"I'll tell ya why. You're the only one who does the cleanup like we told ya. Your area looked better than anyone else's."

Flabbergasted, Jean was at a loss for words. A long, slow minute passed while the Sergeant passed his cap from hand to hand, and looked over his shoulder once again. Jean supposed it was to see if any other officer was nearby.

"Look, if you show the other three guys in your detail today, how you do it, and get all the waste, and burn all the waste, just like so, then I'll let you off the hook for the next coupla days. All right?"

"Sir, yes, sir," Jean all but shouted, once again saluting sharply, feeling relieved, and a little awed over the praise. His mother would be proud. Deep inside, Jean felt proud.

About three days later officers finally lifted most restrictions and some of the men got passes to Salisbury, while others simply slipped away, apparently unnoticed, where they made the usual rounds of inspecting the charming city and finding the nearest pub. Due to the war, the ale was watery, but still tasted good, which was good for the men because shortly after they got orders to leave Druids Lodge for an assigned job.

The 371st headed on June 2nd to Hollington House owned by a wealthy horseman with expensive animals who had offered to house the men in his stables while they transferred and arranged all the supplies likely to be needed after the Allied invasion of France that everyone whispered about, into a nearby engineering depot. Working two shifts to take advantage of the available light, the men loaded barges, Bailey bridges, rail, and thought of their aching shoulders and the coming battle, as increasing numbers of planes droned overhead.

On June 5th the planes in the air reached unbelievable numbers, darkening the skies and creating a looming sense of apprehension as loud as the noise of the engines in the sky. Much speculation as to D-Day's arrival drew down to the early morning of the 6th of June when those hundreds of planes returned to the city, dropping signals and sparks which gave the men hope that the war might be ended before they began their battles. Days of optimism and carefully concealed bets occupied the next week or so.

Although reports over the next months stated that the Allied invasion on Normandy Beach marked a turning point in the war, the other bulletins about sand drenched with blood and bodies, and lifeless forms floating in the waters, turned those glimmering hopes to dust as the soldiers took stock of the huge cost.

Jean and the others whispered softly of an evening over the days ahead about the tragic casualties, and repeated story after story heard in the BBC news or whispered from command that drifted back from France of thousands of brave men lost, injured, or dead. The tension felt palpable. And the fighting to take France back still preoccupied the 371st.

Meanwhile the angry Germans began sending flying bombs to England as part of their new plan to stop the push in France. Civilians evacuated big cities such as London, nearby Coventry, and even Newbury, which took a hit from a stray bomb. Contrasting sharply with the grey skies of war when men on the move witnessed the damage and suffering of the blitz attacks, were the lessons learned about the refined English culture.

In the evenings after work at the depot, or trips to pick up other supplies, the troops took up their posts on bar stoops conversing with the staid British, draining their supplies of ale, and making the pubs the center of social life. Some of the men learned the jitterbug and the hokey pokey in between rounds of beer, and others had invitations to the homes of Englishmen where they flirted with the daughters, respectfully, and learned to admire the courage and generosity of the "stiff, upper lipped" people who dealt with deprivation as if it was nothing, but graciously accepted rations from the soldiers who graced their homes.

The men heard stories of the English taking tea as usual in the bomb shelters during raids, while the china cups rattled in their hands, and explosions drowned out civil conversations. They listened to tales of children doing their lessons by candlelight, amidst the roar of mortar and fire. Visiting soldiers also noticed the increasingly bare pantries, and the rubble of homes and buildings where shopkeepers had once made a decent living. England was ravaged.

Having given up their autos for lack of gasoline, the British use of bicycles for transportation inspired many a soldier to purchase a two-wheeler for his own mode of making social calls or running errands, and even picking up their mailbags.

After five weeks, ratings, promotions, and orders came through. The men prepared to move to Walford House in Taunton traveling on cool, rainy summer days in July, arriving July 9th. Again, their home would be tents, enough to house more than twice the men in their company. The irony that this haunting, empty place had probably been vacated by those soldiers already across the channel, on Normandy Beach, and four other beaches, made for restless sleep that first night. Once again Jean reached into the safe pocket to find his coin, and to swipe his hand over St. Christopher.

Expecting some action the next morning, the men discovered they had to clean up the camp instead, while Headquarters Platoon did basic construction such as plumbing, carpentry, brick work and other repairs on the nearby hospital. As others were out collecting bedding, and cleaning up various camps, HP had two main goals: to finish constructing and remodeling the hospital, and to build an airport and a road from the airfield to the hospital.

Wounded arrived every day from the Normandy front and soldiers felt good about making their travel and housing less hazardous. Some injured, but already improved, arrived unaided, but many, still in their blood soaked uniforms, had to be lifted to the waiting bus or ambulance. Bandages turned brick red from dried blood marked many a man as having that red badge of courage, which Stephen Crane had once written about. Many a soldier they saw gave them pause to thank God for their own location, and to pray or send good thoughts to those elsewhere.

"Poor buggers," Mikey said.

"I hope they all get to go home." Yank whispered.

"Not likely," Ernie said.

"Quieter and cleaner here, at least," said Jean.

"Better care and food, too," Jack added.

"They all deserve medals," Red said, turning away as one man with bandaged eyes came down the new road they had built, pushed on a gurney by Red Cross volunteers.

"At least they have a smooth road now to travel on," Red noted, rubbing his eyes.

"Yes, and real doctors and nurses to finally take care of them," Yank commented.

Still, the unending lines of wounded passed by them on the new paved road they had constructed, moving slowly into the corridors of the remodeled hospital.

Lack of materials sometimes caused delays in the work of construction and a few of the men, friendly with pilots, caught day trips to Ireland or Scotland and back while others took up the sport of gliding, attached to Transports that made their ride thrilling. As the construction sped up, orders came in and some company members transferred to Infantry or Combat Engineers.

Jean learned the motor pool had reorganized into a mobile unit, and his name showed up on that list, so mechanics and drivers began working with their new equipment, painting numerals and the necessary amount of identification stars on vehicles. Jean sometimes drove to get the mail and other supplies, giving him a much needed break from the camp, until he realized when he got back that he had another assignment that evening.

By August 9th the soldiers had seen enough leisure and received orders for a top secret job at Kingsclere airfield where they built a camp for 3000 men, complete with kitchens and latrines out of 250 tents in three days. This helped prepare the 101st Airbourne departure for a drop behind German lines near Paris.

In three days time, and heavily guarded, the 371st set up the camp, began KP duty to cook for and serve the 101st, a swarming group of leathery vets who had already been in Africa, Sicily, and Italy. Tension mounted as the mix of men got down to business, the 371st, working feverishly to aid, and the Airbourne resting, and stripping to the basics: knives, guns, and ammunition. While they waited, news came of the fall of Paris, and even though the building task had been formidable, the 371st now had to dismantle everything. Grateful to see none of the 101st would have to shed blood, the 371st tried not to complain about the tear down.

During this time of going undercover again, hiding from the German blitz, John Steagall, a Company A driver, had the misfortune to be given a false pass, though he did not know it, to test the alertness of the guard at the post. The guard noticed the inauthentic pass and told Steagall to halt the required number of times before shooting at the cab of Steagall's truck, and blowing out his tires. What could have been a disaster, turned out to be just another lesson in being careful at all costs.

Afterward, and moved back to their Salisbury tents, the soldiers relaxed, received passes, and waited. By Aug. 21, about two and a half months after D-Day, the reunited company received orders to work in five different hospitals, doing whatever work headquarters required of their talents, mostly building shelters over walkways between buildings, constructing storage areas, and erecting partitions between beds.

Finishing a day's work, the soldiers had free time, no roll call, no morning bugle, and a taste of freedom in their mouths. Many enjoyed the benefits of the recreation rooms in the hospitals after hours, playing cards, or darts, listening to the radio, exercising, and reading the newspapers. Some even peeked in on the soldiers and conversed quietly. As more and more information became known about the Normandy invasion, whispers grew in the rec room.

"I heard about 160,000 went and half were Americans," Red stated somberly.

"No, the BBC reported that 156,000 went, and only 73,000 were Americans, and 83,000 were Brits and Canadians." Ernie said.

A brief silence marked the tension in the air over these disturbing stats.

"Did you hear that the BBC ran a competition requesting French beach holiday photos to plan for D-Day?" Yank asked presently, looking up from clipping his nails, trying to lighten the mood.

"The BBC also said the war department planned for a full moon at spring tide, on June 5, but had to delay 24 hours due to weather." Jean leaned forward into the conversation.

"Only about 15 % of paratroopers landed in the right place," Mikey shook his head sadly.

"Stars and Stripes says the SAS dropped hundreds of dummies from aircraft on other beaches before the invasion to confuse the Germans," Jack chimed in.

"The BBC also said we sent 7,000 ships, and made the Germans think the invasion was at Calais," Red added.

"They even sent Patton and dummy equipment up there." Jean said.

"Bloody Omaha Beach had almost 4,000 killed or wounded," Mikey read from the latest Stars and Stripes, "and the American unit lost 90 % of their men," Mikey finished, then paused at the dead silence. "But that's just a preliminary estimate."

Taking in all this information, everyone remained silent again for an uncomfortable duration.

"Bloody hell," Jack breathed.

"Do you really think that many died on Omaha alone?" Mikey finally asked the question they had all been pondering.

"I heard it was only 2,500 total," Red said. "That was from BBC."

"Only?" Ernie asked.

When the weight of those words sunk in, the discussion ended.

On September 1st the platoons traveled to Fonthill Gifford, a former headquarters for a British unit. Here, the rumors turned into a new reality. They would leave England and go to France as soon as possible. After a scramble to get packed and ready, with even "gas impregnated clothing," as Ernie later scribbled into his notebook, they boarded trucks with their gear, only to find they didn't have enough room for them all.

A walking party, chosen at random, and including 59 men and one officer from company A, marched four miles to Tisbury where they boarded a train to take them to the staging area in Southampton where, again, they had to wait for further orders. Most of the soldiers chose to go to the movies with the little free time still allotted to them.

After one false start early the next morning, the convey on trucks loaded up again that afternoon, while the walking party got boarded onto busses headed to the Southampton dock. Grey skies and a chilly rain enveloped their departure into the belly of another ship with hydraulic lifts. Most of the men did not get bunks, but slept on deck, in trucks, or sandwiched between piles of equipment. Ernie wrote, "The night aboard was cold and uncomfortable. The ship lay at anchor throughout the night."

On September 7th, the ship departed for the full day's journey across the channel to France where they awoke at dawn on the

8th to a nightmare scene on Utah Beach of a desolate wasteland where their comrades, gone before them, sacrificed blood, life, and battered equipment to the gods of war. Lonely looking, with broken barges and half sunk ships, a barren France welcomed them somberly to its ravaged coastline.

✪ ✪ ✪
CHAPTER 6

France

f their landing in England in early spring had been hopeful, the arrival on French beaches in early fall created an eerie, nostalgic sense of huge loss. While England had been blitzed in pocket urban areas by aerial attacks, and the cities had much devastation, almost all of France had been raped, a brutal, deadly assault that left the land looking hollow and empty, stripped of its dignity, and bare of adornment in the yellowed and browned fall haze.

The expanse of sandy shores still showed evidence of lives lost. Bloody bits of clothing, damaged helmets, an empty boot, and scores of ruined equipment spoke of the terrible price paid by those who had landed on D-Day. Soldiers with imaginations believed they could see the sand strewn with flailing bodies, or hear the crashing waves thrust men floating face down, in and out, with the tide.

Jean scoured the channel they had just travelled, watching the waves sweeping the cold beach, and realized that below the waters offshore, many men and much more equipment lay in darkened depths. It was difficult to put thoughts to words, and many of the newly arrived had tears in their eyes as they looked at one another without needing to speak. Several made the sign of the cross, and a few even dropped to their knees, shivering from the merciless winds swiping at the center of all that cried out for the human condition.

As the trucks rolled off the ships with more and more soldiers disembarking, those already landed turned sorrowfully away, unable to experience the new wave of anguished looks and haunted eyes. A cold gust of air swept the flattened beach, shaking them to their cores, and many cursed under their breaths, before moving up the beach to higher ground, ever watchful of the hidden mines they had been warned to avoid. Mud was everywhere, enveloping the landscape in rivulets of muck, which sucked strongly at their boots.

Company A eventually set up camp shortly after arriving in an open area where a beautiful farm had once graced the previously well manicured Norman territory. The surrounding countryside still bloomed with fruit in the orchards, and ever-mellow cows nibbled nonchalantly on the patches of grass that remained. After a time, young French girls with buckets came to milk the cows, and several of the men chatted with them as the young ladies went about their evening's work, often looking over their shoulders at the soldiers watching them, smiling shyly.

The famous hedge rows that had hidden the German soldiers waiting for the Allies, took on new meaning as Company A realized how their height and depth had been perfect places to watch and wait for the innocently unaware soldier to get closer and closer. Even if many of the landing soldiers shouted back to the others behind them to get down, it had probably been too late. Many of the hedge rows were mangled now from fighting, and ill use, but the once stately picture of grace remained possible to envision.

Once their sleeping tents were erected in the staging area, the men wandered the fields and noted the small and almost intimate links of farm buildings nestled within the green fruit trees, and still somewhat colorful hedgerows not damaged by warfare. Nature had not died, and the happy sight of nearly ripe fruit awakened their appetites to the realization that they were still hungry, and pretty girls milking cows roamed the area next to their camp. Most of the men spent that evening, and well into the next afternoon exploring, eating their fill of fresh fruit, and making new friends.

Late in the afternoon the trucks moved them through 346 kilometers of devastation as they passed near the ruins of St. Lo, Vier, and Alencon, once pretty cities, and stopped near Charlo St. Maas for their next picture of the very real tragedy that had transpired on French soil. Everything looked like broken shells. Their short journey had revealed hundreds of displaced persons, pushing carts or pulling wagons with their earthly possessions. Many waved and smiled, and the guys couldn't help but wonder at the resilience of these people who seemed to have no shelter, but much spirit.

The soldiers threw what little they had left of their rations to the children milling about who were overjoyed to get the "gum, sugar, and bouillon powder, the only tokens they had left," Ernie wrote later that evening after they pitched "their shelter halves, posted guards, and heated up a final can of rations before blackout precautions made it inadvisable, and the men rolled up in blankets on the stubbled ground and tried to sleep."

The next day they were to meet the rest of the Battalion in Etampes at a huge Chateau which had been made into a German headquarters before they were pushed back. Here, Major Jackson, who had taken over for the newly reassigned Colonel Adcock, spoke to the assembled soldiers about how their next movement would take them into the proximity of the enemy's battleground, so they must be aware at all times of what they had learned in basic. Those words brought dead silence to the rows of soldiers listening.

September 11th brought their convoys through 224 kilometers eastward to Vitry le Francois past the outlying reaches of Paris, also heavily damaged, and left with abandoned equipment and shelled out buildings that could be seen from a distance. Everyone did get to view the beautiful cathedral at Rheims, although it still sheltered barricades left to protect it from earlier bombings.

The long lost walking party contacted authorities when they arrived in Utah Beach, but could not find the rendezvous point, and were seriously lost in rain and mud. Lt. Weinstein of A Company ordered the trucks, which had just dropped off the soldiers in Vitry, to return to Utah Beach to pick up the wandering platoon.

By the 14th, the whole company assembled together again at the Marne River where the weary and disheveled looking men at last had a chance to bathe, shave, and wash their clothes on the grassy banks, making good use of the river rocks to clean and dry their uniforms. Many of the men swam and enjoyed the leisurely day, including the truck drivers who washed the mud from their trucks as well.

In their rare downtime, they studied maps, whispered the rumors of stories suggesting misplaced "German troops had been seen in the area, and all were secretly proud of the precariousness of a situation that demanded the carrying of rifles at all times,"

Ernie read to the group gathered around hidden campfires later on in early twilight.

Although no one was allowed to leave camp, a few checked out neighboring debris and empty trenches looking for an elusive bottle of French champagne, which did not turn up. As the evening deepened, the townspeople came out to greet the soldiers and offer to trade their vegetables, wines, and beer for anything of value the soldiers wished to exchange. So a couple of restful days passed.

Jean and the others settled in for their last night in the quiet haven, and talked quietly amongst themselves.

"Never thought I'd get to Europe or to see Paris," Red said.

"I never thought I'd get out of Southern Illinois and mucking horse stalls for the rest of my life," Mikey added.

"History has a way of changing lives," Jack commented.

"You got that right," Yank said.

"What we do might be in history books someday," Jean sat up and leaned into the discussion.

"Well, didn't you learn about WWI in school?" Ernie asked.

"Everything but the dates and places," Jean laughed.

"That's what historians are for," Red chimed in.

"And we've got our historian right here," Mikey said, reaching out and poking Ernie.

"Now, don't go getting full of yourself," Yank said to Ernie with a smile.

"Not me," Ernie answered, ducking his head as Red playfully shadow boxed with him.

On September 16th, the companies received new orders, with Company A going first to an abandoned French army camp, and then to a camp near the village of Sissonne. German soldiers had recently headquartered there, with much evidence of their hasty withdrawal left behind in the stark buildings, an old hospital, and barracks. Company A found personal possessions of the former occupants almost everywhere they looked. Everything from photos to weapons turned up under mattresses and "placards with German sayings such as 'Wo steht den Deusche Soldat, Kommt kein andre dahin.' (Where the German soldier takes his stand, no others come.)" Ernie translated into his journal.

About this time the MPs escorted German POWs into the camp and housed them in small spaces to make guard duty less problematic. The Americans realized soon enough that the POWs had no stomach for going back to their own army, as they began eating well, doing assigned work willingly, and asking for nothing, even though they had been hiding without sleep or nourishment for weeks, and they literally smelled like three weeks of dirt and perspiration.

Jean and the others often noted that, but for the uniform they wore, and the language they spoke, the Germans did not seem much different from them. The engineer unit guarding them must have thought so too, as the POWs had relatively loose leashes, and usually only a couple of guards while they worked or ate. The camp relaxed into a regular routine of almost not noticing their guests of war, except for a shared cigarette and bits of broken conversation.

Company A finally had the opportunity to go into the village of Sissonne and meet the locals who showed them their pubs, and drank wine and champagne with them. Thus began about three days of getting to know their neighbors and drinking their fill, until new orders came in to repair railroads near Charmes and La Fere, including two seriously unsafe bridges shelled by bombs. In quieter times, especially early morning, or in the twilight, they heard the sounds of warfare near Nancy, only a day or so away, reminding them of how close to the front they really were.

The men gradually moved from Camp Sissonne to a large home dubbed the Chateau, which had space for many of the soldiers, but not all. Those inside the walls, by random luck, felt sorry for those forced to sleep outside in the rain and chilly weather. Since time immemorial men have improvised in situations such as these, and many found protection against walls, near garden shrubs, and in straw bedding, as well as in their thick woolen blankets which, wrapped around them, like sleeping blankets, provided double warmth. Later that night before bed, a small group of them huddled together heard Ernie's account from his chronicles, "Without the benefit of a dining room, the men were again messing in the open. Fenders of trucks made good lunch counters."

Meanwhile the company began to help the civilians by working on the demolished railroads and bridges.The Army ordered, and received materials the civilians did not have, to help rebuild the damage. Once that equipment came, the Army pulled back on their efforts to aid in the work, so as to allow the Frenchmen a means to get a paycheck. By September 30th, some of the men went to Etain where they cleared the debris of about forty railroad cars and a locomotive that had been blown up. Most of the men slept in a large barn, but again, many had to camp in the elements.

By October 4th, the whole company gathered and headed east to Stenay, which lay close to the Belgian border. At first they just worked on building a highway bridge 80 feet tall, and repairing the roads around it, but as the weather turned much colder, the large camp and barracks there kept the fireplaces going day and night, requiring much wood. As the bridge and repair work wound down, the hollow feel of the camp and barracks woke up to convoys of more German prisoners arriving.

These POWs would become the basis of Company A's work for many days to come as they began their turn at guarding prisoners. The men found this assignment and the stay in Stenay to their liking, as both the job and the town proved agreeable, a good break from heavy lifting and repairs. In Stenay, Jean found a new sense of brotherhood.

Guarding the Germans brought the topic of *All Quiet* On The Western Front back up in a conversation around one of the fires one night, as his buddies and Jean toasted their toes, and discussed the revelations they had been getting in their dealings with the captured enemy on a daily basis.

"Some of these POWs are younger than we are," Jean said.

"And you're our baby at 18," Ernie teased.

"I'm 19," Jean returned.

"I'm impressed by how much they're like us," Red said.

"That was one of the points made in *All Quiet*," Ernie replied. "The soldiers in that book made the same observation."

"They're our enemy, though," Mikey spoke up.

"Are they, or is it Hitler and the Nazis?" Jack asked.

"I've heard several say they don't want to go back to their own front," Yank added.

"And I've seen a few pictures they carry, family, kids, sweethearts. Just like us," Red responded.

"I don't think they want this war. It's the Nazis and Hitler. They've hypnotized the Germans and the soldiers," Ernie said.

"Really hypnotized them?" Jean asked.

"That march they do? The goose step? It's pretty mesmerizing. Some say that Hitler thinks doing things like that in unison helps brainwash people into believing in the Nazi cause," Ernie stated.

"Like cheering for a team?" Jean asked.

"Isn't that what the Army has us doing too?" Red asked.

"So why are we fighting them?" Mikey asked.

"Good question." Jack said.

"Wars get fought by the grunts like us," Yank replied.

"And we're fighting against Hitler trying to take over the world," Ernie added.

"So the German soldiers are their grunts too," Mikey said.

"Hitler's got to be stopped." Red stated.

"Meanwhile he's safe at home, and these soldiers we're guarding miss their families." Jean said.

"It's a damned shame," Mikey threw in.

The crackling sound of the fire dying down, and the trailing smoke, reminded them that they had early shifts the next day, and they had better get some sleep. As they readied for bed, the quiet sound of the German conversation next door crept through the walls.

"Wish we knew what they were saying," Yank whispered.

"And they probably wish the same about us," Red answered in a low voice.

"Maybe that's why we have wars. After all's said and done, we can't communicate," Jean mused aloud.

Guarding prisoners was hard work, in that it was so boring. Company A had been divided into several groups working three different shifts, so everyone got a little time off after making sure the POWs got fed, cleaned up the camp, including the Honey detail, and got a little exercise before taking care of their personal needs. As they had noted earlier, the prisoners needed little supervision, and seemed happy to do the work asked of them in exchange for food, provisions, and a warm place to sleep. Many soldiers shared their cigarettes or bits of chocolate with the POWs and they were always grateful to get them. The day passed without incident, as most of them did.

CHAPTER 7

The Language of Love

Little did Jean realize that he would learn another language beginning the next day. After shift, he and his buds ate their rations and went into the small town bar near Stenay to drink a few brews and swap lies around a wooden table. The next crew had already taken over the babysitting. At the counter, on a stool at the end of the polished oak bar, sat a young woman with hair the color of dark chocolate, and skin so translucent, it shimmered in the twilight. She was counting coins. She turned, aware of Jean's eyes watching her, and smiled briefly.

Red nudged Jean. "Now's your chance, kid."

"Should I go over?" Jean whispered.

"Why shouldn't you?" Red hissed. The others laughed and resumed their conversation.

Jean grabbed his half full mug, stumbled off his chair and tried to saunter over to the bar. Standing next to her, he smiled and nodded to the empty stool. "You mind?"

She smiled again and he took that as a yes. Jean had taken four years of French in school and he tried to muster up a greeting. She sensed his hesitation and said, "I speak some English." Her voice, a mixture of soft French, and fairly good English, melted his heart.

He sat down, their arms touched, and they both smiled. Jean leaned in. "You have captured my interest, mademoiselle."

"We are happy you captured the German soldiers who were stealing our poultry," she returned, with a grin, with lights dancing in the depths of her dark eyes.

"I'm sorry," Jean said, "Forgot my manners. My name's Jean."

"I'm Merie," she replied, "and thank you for coming to France to protect us."

Just then the bartender came down from the other end of the bar, and said, "Merie, you'd best get home before dark." She introduced Jean to the bartender. "Papa, this is Jean."

Her father nodded to Jean and then said, "Come back again for breakfast tomorrow, Jean. Merie brings fresh eggs from our farm and cooks for us daily."

"I have guard duty tomorrow. Is it ok if I walk your daughter home instead?"

The man looked at Jean, while he absent-mindedly swiped out a glass with a white towel. Jean assumed Papa might be mentally counting in his head that the soldier had only had one beer, the first one, not even finished. "All right, and then come to dinner tomorrow night at our home. I'm off tomorrow." He looked at Merie, "Go on, then, and don't forget your tips."

"Thank you, sir, and thanks for the invitation. I'd be happy to come." Jean was thinking, in spite of himself, a beautiful girl, and real food. "I wouldn't miss it."

"When does your duty end tomorrow?" The Papa asked.

Jean told him. The barkeep added an hour to Jean's shift ending, and told him to go straight to the farm. "You'll know where it is, then."

Jean stood, shook hands with Papa, and turned to Merie who was sweeping the shiny silver into a small cloth purse. "G'Nite, Papa," she said, waving, as Jean took her elbow and escorted her past his buds, who couldn't help but stare at him. He smirked over his shoulder, and they went out the door, its little bell jingling their exit.

Thus began Jean's foray into really learning French, and another language he had only tasted briefly, in a few lingering kisses he had shared with girls from school back home when he gave them rides, every once in a while, in one of Irish's cabs.

That night, when he got back to camp, all eyes turned to Jean. It was about 9:30 and they had apparently had a few more beers. "C'mon, give," Red said.

Jean had thought about this on the way back. He didn't want to kiss and tell, but he had to say something. He looked at Ernie.

"Did you at least get a good night's kiss?" Ernie prodded gently.

"I walked her home, she introduced me to her mother, her sisters, and brother, and then we sat on the porch and talked," Jean said quietly.

"Oh then, no kiss," Yank probed, waving his hands.

Jean smiled, pulled his shirt over his head, paused, then said, "A couple."

Everybody hooted and clapped him on the back. Jean hadn't felt this good since the last time he had caught a fish.

The next morning, they all dragged themselves out of bed and went back to guard duty. Jean couldn't wait to get himself back to the quiet farm for dinner, and to see beautiful Merie, and he seemed a little impatient, checking the time whenever possible. The others teased him all day, and Jean tried to be good natured, but they were making him nervous.

"Dinner with Papa and the whole family already…" Red taunted.

"Should we publish banns of marriage in the church bulletin?" Yank said as seriously as he could.

"Ah, leave him alone," Ernie stated.

"But you'll tell us all about it, won't you," Mikey asked.

"You bet he will," Jack said, slapping Jean on the back.

After the changing of the guard, and some washing up, Jean started off on his walk to the farm, wondering what he'd have for dinner, and whether the meal would take long. He knew he'd be subjected to lots of questions, and he had already promised his mother in his head that he'd help clean up, and be sure to thank them all graciously.

Things couldn't have gone more smoothly if he'd scripted a screenplay. Merie's parents, two sisters, and Merie herself made him feel very welcome. The younger brother was missing, taking Papa's place in the bar. For dinner they had a scrawny baked chicken, toasted to an appetizing golden brown, with real potatoes, late garden vegetables, and fresh bread. Jean couldn't say whether he liked the food or the company better. Their questions didn't bother him at all, as they merely wanted to know about his life, and about living in the States.

Those things he talked about with ease. His family, schooling, driving the cabs, and growing up as an all American boy seemed to interest them too much so he decided to switch gears, and ask them some tough questions about their recent experiences.

Sitting with their wine and a little fruit and cheese for dessert, Jean asked about how the war had affected their family. Listening to their stories, he was struck by the poignant resignation they all seemed to have at being overtaken by the Germans, and their particular dislike of the fall of Paris. Most of their exchanges with the Germans had been without incident, but they mourned the loss of much of the food they had canned for the winter, as the Germans had raided their pantries, as well as their poultry.

After eating and then clearing the table, Jean and Merie headed toward the sink. Mama spoke up. "Let your sisters do the dishes, Merie. You and Jean go milk the cows and put the chickens to bed."

Papa settled by the fire, his feet propped on an ottoman. "We want a full report when you've finished," he said, taking up the open book on the table by the chair. Jean realized for the first time why Papa was not in this war. Under his pants, a wooden leg on the stool made Jean look up and meet Papa's eyes.

"WWI," Papa said.

The next morning, Jean got razzed by the others. "What time did you get in?" Mikey asked, yawning widely.

"Early," Jean said, pulling his socks up. "Early this morning." Everyone laughed.

Throughout the day, he answered their questions about the meal, the family, and how he did milking the cows, and chasing the chickens. He told them about getting squirted in the eye with milk, almost getting kicked by a cow with too full, tender udders, and how the chickens seemed to find it fun to escape going to bed. They wanted to know if he got any more kisses too. Jean replied honestly but with precision, as they supervised the POWs throughout the day, and every spare minute, Jean remembered the feel of Merie's mouth under his probing lips. Unfortunately, their full report had to eventually be given to Papa and so everyone had sat around the fire talking until Merie's brother came in after the bar closed a little after midnight.

"Papa has a car that needs to be tuned up, and I'm going over there tomorrow to work on that," Jean said. "Guess I'll have to take tonight off, and catch up on my sleep."

So the weeks passed, and Jean began to feel he had a second family. Once, when Mikey asked how old the sisters were, Jean told him quickly. "Too young. They're only 12 and 14." He already felt protective of 18 year old Merie, and of her family. He really liked the brother Henri, too, who was two years younger than Jean, and not old enough for war. Merie's Mom was an older version of her daughter, open, honest, and refreshingly sweet. And Papa, Papa was a good father.

Mixed in with guard duty during the days, his nights became a second refuge at the farm. Not only did he finally get the car running smoothly, washed up, and waxed, he also learned to churn sweet cream into rich soft butter, how to make a flakey pie crust from scratch, and helped to fix up the things around the farm that needed mending. He rebuilt fences, repaired broken windows, and, together with Merie's help, winterized the little house for the coming winter, putting burlap over the north windows and door, and plastic over the other sides of the compact little farm.

He did not go for supper every night, knowing they had real need of their food, but often they played board games inside, or horseshoes and other games outside, if it wasn't too chilly, and whenever he could, Jean brought them soap, bits of chocolate and gum. They teased him with their conversations in French until they realized he could understand bits and pieces pretty well from his days taking French in school. They made it a game then, teaching him what he didn't know. They still milked the cows and bedded the chickens, and sometimes, he and Merie went for walks. He looked forward to the walks most of all.

The weather grew increasingly colder and they bundled up to go out under the stars and moon, and talk about anything and everything. Jean watched Merie as she spoke, her animation engaging his interest, and her beauty capturing his heart more and more each time he saw her. One night she ran off, and began hiding behind trees, playing a seductive kind of grown-up hide and seek. He watched her, in her farm girl overalls, with a heavy sweater covering, but not quite hiding her shapely curves, careen out of sight momentarily, and then reappear behind another tree close by. He loved to see her lithe body move, and her full figure taunt him as much or more than her pretty face, bright mind, and happy spirit.

Chasing her, finally catching her into his arms, they held each other as if they would never let go, and when he kissed her, all time stopped, and, as they breathlessly let go of each other, came up for air, and gazed into each other's eyes, he knew this happiness could not continue. Already rumors were circulating their camp, that another unit would soon take over guard duties, and Company A would cross over into Belgium. He didn't know how he could leave her, and that night Jean decided to write a letter to his own Papa.

Putting the tip of the pencil to his lips, thinking about what to write, Jean didn't notice Mikey come up behind him, quietly looking over his shoulder.

"Writing poems, now?" Mikey teased. When he saw the blank paper, he laughed. "Deep thoughts, buddy."

"Writing home," Jean said with an air of annoyance. He was thinking whatever happened to privacy.

Ernie looked up from his journal. "Want me to read what I've written about you and Merie?" He asked with a straight face.

Jean stood and reached for the spiral notebook. "You didn't. You wouldn't," he said as he tried to grab the book from Ernie.

Ernie saw the betrayed look in Jean's eyes, and he noted a vulnerability he remembered having felt himself once, all too well, so he handed his notes to Jean. "No, just kidding."

Jean looked, then turned and sat on the far side of his own bed and began to write. Much later, he read his letter, addressed it to his father, put it in an envelope, sealed it, placed it in his duffel, and went to bed. He would mail it, first chance. Everyone else was already asleep.

The next morning, one of the POWs was vomiting, and everyone convened to discuss the best treatment. Searching their motherly advice banks, the men came up with fluids, chicken soup, and lots of hand washing so no one else got sick. It didn't work. The germs flew about the camp, and at least a third of the POWs, constrained together most of the time in their own smaller barracks, got sick, and probably a fourth of the guards came down with something similar. By the end of the week, all their chicken bouillon cubes had been used, and most everyone was on the mend.

Merie showed up at their camp on day three of the beginning of the sickness with a bottle of vinegar and told Jean to cleanse everything they all touched with vinegar diluted in water to disinfect. Jean realized the extent of his feeling for her as she explained she had heard about the illness in the camp from the few men who were still well enough to go to the pub and drink or eat there. He kissed her briefly when she finally turned to go, and the whole camp broke into applause. Embarrassed, Jean walked with her a short distance, and gave her a longer kiss down the road, out of sight of the soldiers. When he got back to camp, everyone was talking about how the vinegar seemed to be helping already, and Ernie remarked, "Well, it took care of the. Black Plague." Everyone laughed. Jean was just glad that no one was still talking about his stolen kiss.

Dream of drowning

That night Jean dreamed that he was floundering in a deep pool of water, and trying to rise to the surface. He was finally able to break through and catch a breath of air. He took a deep cleansing breath and gasped as he finally was able to breathe normally. He thought about what this dream might mean and could come up with nothing. The next morning he remembered the dream, and pondered it before the bugle sounded. When the call to wake up finally sounded, the thought came to him that he must do something about losing Merie. He reached into his backpack, took the letter out and put it on top of his backpack so that he could remember to mail it as soon as possible.

After dressing, roll call and breakfast, which seemed to take forever, Jean was able to get back to the barracks and retrieve his letter and drop it in the mailbox. He suspected he would be assigned to drop off the mail in the nearest town later that day. A great weight lifted from his shoulders.

After he finally dropped off the letter in the mailbox in the next town over, he began the long wait for the answer to his hopes and dreams.

The next morning they did indeed get orders to move to Belgium. That night he had to tell Merie they were leaving in two days and he didn't know when he would be back as the companies took turns guarding the POWs. While they waited, he made the most of every moment he could get with Merie and held her as if each time would be the last. When she showed up to camp just as they were leaving and waved to him, he felt the blur of tears in his eyes. He said good bye to her with a long lingering kiss, gathered up his belongings, not caring that the others had whooped and whistled when he kissed Merie and ignoring their pats on his back. As they began their trek to Belgium, he turned for one long, last look at Merie and he saw that she too was crying.

Belgium

The Germans had first landed in Belgium in early May of 1940, with the intent of using it as a gateway to invading France and then overtaking the rest of western Europe. The Americans arrived too late to stop them from invading France. However, they were finally able to push the Germans further and further to the southeastern corner of Belgium.

It wasn't until October 12, 1944, that the Captain of Company A got orders to move the company northeast to Ciney, Belgium located in the province of Namur. Later that night, Ernie wrote in his journal, "Looking more than ever like big city scavengers than part of an army, the outfit squeezed into its trucks and headed northeast...The change from France to Belgium, with its low rounded scenic mountains abundantly covered with forest, was also extreme in the sense that the people seemed not as poverty stricken by the effects of the war."

Though he had no heart for moving on, Jean soon found that the people of Belgium were so jovial and welcoming that he could not help but be cheered. The soldiers were divided into four groups. The Headquarters claimed a large, empty chateau for themselves. Four days later when the second platoon finished their work on the railroads in France and came to Belgium to rejoin the company, they found a second Chateau ready and waiting for their arrival. Sergeant Wayne's third platoon settled in a monastery, and, Ernie commented wryly, "The berobed brethren offered sharp contrast to the swearing, helmeted Engineers."

The first platoon called an old theater behind a tavern their new home. One of the men living in the theater commented to Ernie who later wrote about it in his journal "They slept in the balcony, on the auditorium and stage, its dressing rooms, and found sanctuary beneath the stage itself...Sergeant Wayne's men had a good home in the monastery, but the 1st platoon, besides having to sleep amongst theater seats, stacks of boxes and other stored items, found the roof to be a hopeless sieve, and when the long days of rain, which seemed the source of Belgium's fall weather, came, came also roaring complaints. With buckets crowding the floor, mopping a continual necessity, and their own initiative their only resort, they covered the roof with tarpaulins. However the aged theater had her blessings as well as hardships and rewarded the men with 83 bottles of fine cognac... packed beneath the steps leading to the balcony back stage."

Not long after finding their new treasure, the soldiers got a good look at how the Black Market worked. Due to the heavy damage and loss the Belgians had suffered during the German occupation, most of their prices were exorbitant compared to what the men had found in France. The shopkeepers often invited soldiers into their homes in compensation for the price gouging. One of the shopkeepers, whose store Jean frequented often, extended a standing invitation for meals at his home with his family of four. His daughter, who was engaged, also had, according to local custom, her fiancé living with the family under the chaperoning eyes of her parents and her snoopy brother. This tradition could last anywhere from six months to a year depending on the outcome of the couple living together and getting to know all of each other's quirks. Jean thought it a charming custom and was amused to witness the look on the future groom's face as he watched his bride-to- be come down to the kitchen for breakfast in her bathrobe and hair rollers. These incidents, when he was not on duty, distracted Jean from his longing for Merie but also made him realize how much he missed her. Still he enjoyed the family meals immensely, the atmosphere, and the relative ease with which they welcomed him into their little circle.

When he was not at the shopkeeper's home, on his off duty hours, he went with many of the other soldiers to visit the famous sights of the small country known for its amusing mannequin piss sculpture, chocolate, lace, warm atmosphere and convivial gatherings at pubs during the evening hours. On one of their tours, the soldiers were impressed with the churches of the city and surrounding areas. The Belgians were as warm and generous as the French had been if not even more so.

While on duty, Jean had little time to think except on the long motor pool trips he took to deliver and pick up mail and to drop off scouts to assess the proximity of the German army. While the scouts were busily taking notes and calculating distances, and noting where they thought they saw evidence of German encampments, Jean went into reveries about Merie. Once in awhile he was interrupted by talk slightly louder than normal, which drew him away from his daydreams, when the scouts discovered something they did not know or had not expected. Their reports would bring exciting news back to the camp that night and would engage him completely in conversations with the other soldiers about next anticipated maneuvers.

On the whole, the war interested him greatly, as being of German ethnicity himself, and had several times been stopped and scrutinized as a spy by Nazi soldiers who tried to act non assertively while roaming the streets of the cities freely to gather information. He felt a great deal of empathy, not only for the Western World, but also a little guiltily for the common ordinary everyday folks like the Germans in his own family who had emigrated to the United States in the 1800s to escape earlier German wars. Many of the Germans in Germany today probably wished they has done the same thing, but having been caught up in the rapidly escalating surge to power by the Third Reich, had found themselves unable to do so.

Later that night, he went back to his little family where their reality amused him. He watched the groom-to-be gaze with astonishment as his darling future bride installed hair rollers in preparation for bed so that she would look beautiful for him the next morning. Nothing like seeing the routine to bring a dash of reality to future life, Jean thought to himself. He almost spit out his sip of coffee as that thought ran through his mind.

His other customary duties included joining the whole company's overall job in Ciney to make improvements to the hospital that the Germans had built and abandoned before it had even been used, because the Allies had pushed them back eastward. Captain Simmons' men specifically built a weather proofed tent with quarters big enough to provide care for the current convalescents and medical employees. The rows of the tent annex, walled with wood sidings and doors, included stoves, electricity, running water and even plumbing. This section required a good deal of carpentry which Jean's platoon mostly managed having themselves been taught by fathers who were carpenters. Working next to the plumbers, the carpenters took out a wall spanning two floors where plumbers added more lavatories on the outside of the wall.

With these enhancements to the hospital nearly finished, the third platoon left Belgium for Avancourt to build railway spurs in links from 1,000 to 1,800 feet, and constructed stands for a supply dump between them. While Lieutenant Weinstein's second platoon, including Jean, went to St. Hubert to build a sawmill to supply the Seventh Army. Back at the hospital Sergeant Victory's men continued installing a prisoner stockade in preparation for the arrival of POWs to do supervised details around the hospital. Thus, all the men had general and specialized duties. Late one night, a group of Jean's buddies sat around complaining about the long days and short nights.

"What do you hate the most about being in the war?" Jack queried.

Jean immediately replied, "I never get enough sleep. And I never get enough to eat."

Ernie added, "I never get enough time to write."

Mikey simply said, "I miss my horses."

Yank threw up his hands and responded, "Everything!"

Red ended the conversation on a note that made everyone laugh, "I never get enough time to chase women."

On the larger front, the Germans plagued England with buzz bombs interrupting daily lives. Due to Ciney's location directly within the pathway between the German trajectory and their targets across the English Channel, the men in Ciney felt the reverberations from the bombing raids, reminding the soldiers of their much safer location. The platoons had some short periods after they completed their major assignment to shop in the city of Ciney buying such gifts as perfume and other trinkets to send home to their parents, family members and sweethearts for Christmas. Jean noticed an artist's stand with its easel and the artist conveniently stationed at a busy intersection. Sitting idly, at least for the moment, the artist beckoned to Jean.

"How about a portrait to send home to your mother? I will give you a good price and catch the character of your impish face." This tickled Jean and so he asked how much?

The artist haggled with him shortly over the cost and Jean due to the shortage of cigarettes and his lack of interest in smoking noticed the ash tray by the artist's easel. With very little negotiation, he was able to lower the price considerably by offering the artist his whole ration of smokes.The artist held up several example of sizes and different media from which to choose. Jean decided to splurge on an 11X14 pencilled drawing for his mom and dad. And at the last minute said, "Could you do a much smaller wallet sized picture included in the same price?"

"You have a lot of cigarettes there. I think I could manage that if you throw in a few bars of soap." Soap was also a much needed item in the city. The Black Market had its plusses as well as its evils. Jean realized how much Europe had suffered from the war to endure the loss of such daily pleasures and necessities.

When he saw the finished portraits, his eyes opened wide in astonishment. He felt as if he were looking in a mirror and raved to the artist about his accomplishment. "I told you, I do good work," the artist replied with a sly smile. Jean was thinking he might be able to find a way to send the small picture to Merie.

The newly built plumbing replaced the famous "honey pot" detail of cleaning latrines and cheered all the men. Keeping the tent area as tidy as possible, hearing constant updates about future maneuvers, (as much as the brass could tell them), and other simple daily routines like eating and sleeping, kept Jean from being sad and missing Merie. Life went on. Sometimes surprising things happened. Headquarter's guards would always remember a small Belgian girl bringing them a delicious bowl of soup almost every day at lunch.

While they were in Belgium the holiday of Thanksgiving rolled around and mail arrived bringing treats from home. Jean also got the dreaded reply to his letter written earlier to his dad. His answer was a resounding, "No! Do NOT bring that French girl home." That put a severe damper on Jean's mood.

Belgians again in thanks for their increased revenue demonstrated their thankfulness by decorating the soldiers' festive, food-filled tables with bottles of free fine wine in honor of Thanksgiving. Later that night when the soldiers had their fill of their celebration feast, Brass provided them a wonderful show at the hospital featuring the long legged husky voiced Marlene Dietrich. The men rejoiced not only over seeing such a fine looking woman, but also over the generosity of beautiful stars like this one willing to donate their time to give them something more satisfying to think about. The next day the soldiers went back to work after many of them had dreamed about a sexy girl with a raspy voice and woke up refreshed. That made it easier to finish up the details renovating the hospital.

Meanwhile the weather began to promise late autumn rains. Working outside caused new problems including trench foot cropping up among all the troops including the Engineers.

Two days after Thanksgiving Lieutenant Schuster and his men also completed building the stockade at the hospital and received the assignment to go back to Stenay to take their turn guarding the new influx of POWs, which required the members of the company to rebuild a more substantial enclosure. Before Schuster's men left for Stenay, Jean took the opportunity to draw aside a man he knew slightly, entrust him with the small portrait of himself and ask him to please track down Merie at her Papa's pub and give it to her. "Tell her that I will love her forever," Jean said. The man agreed to do his best. Jean replied sternly, "Please do better than that." The soldier placed the precious picture in the top pocket of his shirt, closed the button and patted it securely. Jean nodded his thanks. He stewed about if or when to tell Merie about his father's response.

Back in Ciney, Headquarters held down the fort alone doing the finishing details and completing their work by November 30th before moving to Poix St. Hubert where they added their strength to the numbers of other soldiers constructing the sawmill in their always muddy boots. Of course, Headquarters found another old Chateau near St Hubert to call home. That entire area covered with beautiful forestation, reminded the Americans they were getting closer to the Ardennes located between Belgium, Luxembourg, Germany and France, which was where the Allies believed the Germans to be more concentrated. A cascading waterfall flowed beautifully throughout the landscape of the Chateau helping to make it an ideal and restful place. However, the dampish weather continued making the work at the sawmill a muddy mess. Again the soldiers lucked out and found a generous supply of cognac in the village pub which helped alleviate their woes.

Lieutenant Duren returned his third platoon to aid the second platoon, but stayed just two days before being assigned to Stenay. Jean asked Duren, whom he knew slightly from the motor pool, to see if he could find out if the picture had been delivered to Merie mentioning the courier's name at the last minute.

In the meantime the second platoon continued pouring concrete for foundations, reworked the roads to make them more passable, and placed machinery where needed. The Company finally found some downtime after finishing up the small details including installation of electricity, to do some good hunting for Christmas which was coming up. Everything started to come into place when the men saw deer slipping out of their cover for water, "a sight to thrill the heart of any hunter," Ernie commented and jotted down in his notebook. On one of those fortuitous occasions, Ed Breault tracked the deer up into the forest with three other men taking cover amongst the foliage, holding their rifles in position, and waited. Eventually, two young bucks showed up in Breault's sights who took a shot and the deer fell.

Along came a Belgian game warden in his uniform and cap after hearing the echo of the shot higher up the hill. After investigating that the deer had been killed, he arrested them and took them and the deer in a truck to fill out the necessary forms. The men agreed to share the cost of the $100 fine imposed, but the warden dropped the charges after negotiating with the army. The soldiers later dressed the deer back at the Chateau's kitchen, helped by the mess sergeant. Other interested onlookers crowded around offering help and suggestions on how to present the dark, wild meat on a mess gear. Ernie later wrote about this excitedly in his journals.

Christmas spirit spurred the men's excitement as presents

started to show up about a week before the holiday. The men planned a party with decorations and all the trimmings, but a German plan nixed all that by breaking through in Belgium. Growing concern in the troops as civilians already began leaving their homes for more western highways. Rumors abounded as some civilians stayed to monitor the information circulating in the army. One such piece of intel they overheard the soldiers say suggested the 101st Airborne at Bastogne needed ammunition. They scouted neighboring troops and took possession of any munitions including Company A's bazookas.

German attacks increased in frequency calling for scouts to make dangerous trips between Company A and the battalion. These resulted in the decision to abandon the site at the Chateau since the unit had no real defenses to make a stand.

Later that night, Ernie wrote in the chronicles, "The portion of Company A at Poix St Hubert, (the 3rd and 1st platoons still being at Stenay) left December 20th with the rumors of German troops driving toward St Hubert itself. Stories of wildest proportions were coming from civilians, and with the departure of the Company, the village at Poix, already desolate was empty except for a handful of those few who evidently had no fear for the Nazi.

The roar of guns which could often be heard in the distance now had come close indeed. A part of Headquarters platoon had left the previous afternoon to make arrangements for the entire company in Sedan, and, with rumors now coming in of paratroopers and tanks spearheading in their direction, the men who remained until December 20th had an uneasy wait. Any man who has stood guard duty on such a cold, pitch dark night can assure his buddies it is no effort to stay awake. Even when the next day came it was necessary to call for volunteers to remain behind a little longer to destroy equipment and supplies, and remove machinery from the sawmill."

When they first arrived in Sedan tired and weary from their long, cold journey, knowing they had yet to face the Nazis, the men joked about how nice it would be to snuggle and cuddle with the sexy female Santa, full sized, who wore only a red stocking cap, whom they had named Christmas Eve. Unfortunately, somewhere along the way from Poix St Hubert where they had prepared a Christmas celebration to Sedan, she had mysteriously disappeared. No one had ever been able to find her. The men laughed, remembering how much they had enjoyed her for the short time they had her until some selfish pervert or perverts had stolen her. They all had a good laugh wondering which one among them was the pervert who stole her to keep for himself.

CHAPTER 9

The Ardennes:
The Battle the Bulge

Arriving in Sedan, located in the Ardennes, Company A found the same hustle and bustle they had experienced two days before in St. Hubert. Civilians packing up their belongings, tried to stay out of the paths of threatening convoys already filling the streets. Nazi Troops prepared their defenses and in two days had made the Sedan a heavily fortified area. Company A's scout sent ahead from St Hubert found Company B still occupying their quarters. Contrary to the rumors that B had just cleared out, the rest of the Company just hours behind the scout now received a message the Chateau in Sedan was still in Company B's possession. As late as it was, the tired group decided they would just try to get a little sleep finding spaces to throw sleeping gear on the basement floor of the once beautiful mansion. All the men coming in from the snow and cold first gathered as close to the furnace as possible and decided to wait until dawn to find roomier housing to accommodate both Company A and B.

Before they settled down to sleep, a few of the soldiers opened Christmas packages recently received before departing St. Hubert. They also covered windows, secured precarious light for some of the not so tired men to play poker, while others ate rations, and the lucky ones savored the good stuff that had been in their packages. The Companies, exhausted and unsatisfied with the hastily thrown together, move finally all went to sleep.

At dawn Lieutenant Huddleston checked out the upheaval in Sedan and reported to his men upon his return to the crowded basement that their quarters might not provide them the room they needed, but would serve until they could find better housing. Huddleston thought one possibility might be a nearby Chateau enclosed by a moat at Rubicourt five kilometers from Sedan. First he wanted to send a group of three scouts to check out its safety. Later the scouts assured Huddleston that the Chateau would give them both the privacy and security they needed. Both Companies moved again to their new quarters the next day. After this relocation in the penetrating cold, they were disappointed that although the Chateau could hold the 210 men somewhat comfortably, the old mansion had no heat nor lights.

Headquarters immediately assigned the second and third platoons who had just come in from Stenay, the job of building a bridge across the River Meuse in the heart of Sedan. The previous structure, bombed out by the Germans, had been hastily replaced by the Combat Engineers, but proved too unsteady to hold the heavy loads it carried. The Company had directions to construct a bridge right next to it able to carry at least 100 tons. The others, not working on the new bridge, assisted the two way traffic by turning away vehicles with heavy loads.

However, their short stay at Rubicourt provided much excitement as the Germans sent spies dressed in American uniforms seeming to possess valid IDs. They also had American equipment, army vehicles, army munitions, and spoke good English. The Allies heavily guarded all cross points and checked everyone who looked even a little shady. Night travel, particularly uneasy, kept soldiers awake and on their toes. Super conscious MPs and guards stopped all soldiers who even looked remotely anxious, as they had received intel concerning several incidents of ambush.

On December 23rd, the courier Tom Cremins and his driver Jean Etzel returned to the Company, their jeep loaded with bags of Christmas mail when the two soldiers had the scariest experience of their lives.

After Cremins and Etzel finally returned after giving their account of what had happened to the brass, Ernie took Jean aside who was still quite shaken and said, "Tell me what happened so I can write it in the notebook." Jean, calling Cremins over to Ernie and explaining about the historian's chronicles, asked his partner in their near death experience if he could help tell Ernie the story. Cremins, seeming a little calmer than Etzel, readily agreed and they huddled with Ernie in a corner and recounted their ordeal.

After having some chow later that night and Jean had almost quit trembling, Ernie read from his notebook to all the men gathered around to listen to his account of what had happened.

"Cremins was sitting high on the mail bags trying to be as comfortable as possible in the cold night wind (the top having been taken off the jeep to accommodate the load) when he and Etzel noticed another jeep stopped in the road ahead. Suspicious themselves, they slowed only a little and attempted to get by. They sideswiped the vehicle and spun to a stop in the road just beyond.

The occupants of the suspicious jeep threw a hand grenade without saying a word. The two Company A men heard the fuze, thanked the stars the top was off their jeep, and plunged for a ditch. The grenade exploded harmlessly at a distance, but the strangers immediately opened fire with carbines and only after firing a dozen rounds did they call for a surrender. Perhaps, they had heard the frantic shouting by the mail man, 'We're Americans,' above the noise. The two men were asked the password, and not knowing it, were fired on again, but further pleading won them a chance to come forward and be recognized. Skeptical but in view of the fact another vehicle was arriving on the scene, they advanced as instructed, hands over head and found their assailants Americans, men from a non-combatant outfit placed on special patrol duty, nervous and hasty in their judgment. Officers in the third jeep to enter the scene aided in the identifications. Another approaching vehicle, its driver hearing shots and seeing the disturbance ahead, turned in its tracks and went the way it had come. Military police were notified and towed Company A's battered jeep and courier to the company area. The men were pale with fright, but whole. Their jeep, however, had a dozen bullet holes through its windshield and engine. The mail was saved."

The room turned eerily quiet as Ernie looked up and took a breath.

"Wow!" Red interjected, "Sounds like you almost lost your family jewels tonight, Jean."

All the men laughed breaking the tension in the room. Even Jean had to smile at that remark. When the comic relief broke, the men began to ask Jean some serious questions.

"How did you prove you were Americans?" Mikey asked.

"It took some doing," Jean replied. Jean went on, "Cremins answered that he was from Chicago. When they asked him, who won the National League in football, he told them and they were satisfied. Then they asked me where I was from. I said Rock Island, Illinois."

"And of course, he never heard of that, did he?" Yank asked.

"Of course not. I told him it was about 3 hours away from Chicago, and he seemed somewhat satisfied with that."

"Then what did he ask you?" another bystander asked.

Jean replied, "He asked me who won the World Series in baseball," Jean threw up his hands in the air, "I told him 'I don't follow sports. I have no idea!' Then he asked me to show him how I hold my utensils when I eat. I said 'What the _____ !' I had no idea why he wanted to know that."

A bystander asked, "Did he tell you why he wanted to know?" A buzz of small talk broke out among the men gathered around. In response to the jumble of all the noise and commotion, Ernie held up his hand signaling for quiet.

Jean continued, "Yeah.. He said Europeans and Americans eat differently. So I held up my pretend fork and my pretend knife and said, 'Now what?' He told me to pretend to cut my meat on my plate." Jean demonstrated by shifting his fork to his left hand to spear the meat and sawing it with his knife in his dominant right hand.

Ernie said, "I think the Europeans eat differently."

"Yeah, they do. They pile the food on their fork and deliver it to their mouth." The bystander verified. And Ernie nodded.

Jean again threw up his hands in exasperation. "I had no idea."

About then, Cremins sauntered in picked up on the tail end of the conversation and said, "You think you got interrogated." Cremins sat down, "I spent about two hours giving my report to the MPs and the brass, told them everything. They kept asking question after question and finally, the brass sternly scolded me,'You realize how worried you had us, don't you? You were more than three hours late getting back here. And things are getting really dangerous out there. We had to call for volunteers from your company to move to the front line to blow up bridges being built to connect the city and roads. German planes have bombarded us at the front with flak and anti-aircraft fire to keep the company from the bridges. Fortunately, their aim wasn't good. The German bombs didn't fall where they planned and caused no real damage. Still the Germans sent a single pilot whom we named Bedcheck Charlie to drop a stray bomb off and on without warning.'

Cremins continued, "I told him we lost complete track of time because of the confusion and I had no idea you were worried or this was going on, or I would have radioed in. Our hands were still over our heads with guns pointed at us."

Cremins looked at the group gathered around and asked, "Did any of you know that all this was going on?" The bystanders were all shaking their heads no and saying things like, "I had no clue…Nobody told me…This must have been really top secret stuff behind the scenes…"

Ernie added, "They probably only asked a few volunteers so as not alarm the rest of us." The room went quiet.

Cremins shook his head and said, "Wow! No wonder everyone was so suspicious. They could have forewarned us so we might have been a little more careful." Cremins dropped his head into the palms of his hands, "I am just about all done in."

Jean in a weary voice said, "I have got to get some sleep and so do you. Why don't we just call it a night?" The group broke up into smaller groups and drifted away talking among themselves.

Jean lay in bed that night and began to tremble again, the full realization of what had almost happened to him finally sinking in. He ruminated over it a good long time before he felt Ernie's hand reach over, pat him gently on the arm and say, "It's OK to be afraid. Now let it go and get some sleep."

Too early the next morning, the bugle call awakened the soldiers, who now truly felt like soldiers and brought them back to their basic routine of reveille, roll call, regular exercises to wake them up (which they really needed that morning), and breakfast. While eating their chow, they heard rumors that a second group had been sent out to stave off the Germans attack on the bridge near the River Meuse and their soldiers. They also heard they would want nighttime volunteers that evening to take over the second shift. As the Christmas holiday approached, the German drive touched many of the troops but spared Company A who chalked up no casualties. The bulk of the attacks the Germans concentrated on platoons 1 & 3 still working in Stenay on the prison stockade. This structure had been enlarged to sections that held around 2,000 German POWs some in tents, others in the original old French Fort. They received the bulk of the attacks, caught in night raids on their own POWs perhaps because the Germans did not want the prisoners giving away any information, or maybe because the lights simply provided a good target. Finally, the Captain simply ordered the floodlights off completely.

The attack that caused the most damage came on New Year's Eve when the Germans sneakily set off a series of cluster bombs and attacked the area repeatedly with machine gun fire from low flying aircraft. The German POWs incurred four dead and 16 wounded. Fifteen of the Allies received wounds, one fatal.

Still the work on the stockade continued. The prisoners did most of the work thankful to have some cover from their own men shooting at them. Shortly before the New Year's Eve raid, the third platoon packed up and went from Stenay to Sedan. There they reported on the happenings in Stenay particularly at Panama Hatty's still busy as ever. This caught Jean's attention as it was Merie's Papa's pub. While the returning men bragged about the cognac they had enjoyed there, Jean interrupted and asked if anyone had seen Merie, the barkeep's daughter. No one seemed to remember her and this made Jean muse over the reason why. After several scary scenarios took place in his mind, he settled on the conclusion that Papa had been keeping his daughter safe at home from the raids.

After New Year's with the ruthless raiding by the Germans on Stenay, the German power gave out. This was further confirmed by scouts from Company A standing at the top of a high bluff surveying the nearby bridge. Then they scanned where they had been told the German's approximate location would be. They were looking through a pair of binoculars far off into the distance. Jean saw through the binoculars a Panzer being pulled by what looked like horses.

"Well would you look at that," exclaimed Jean handing the binoculars off to Yank next to him.

Yank looked out over the far away landscape and saw the same scene. They were trying to calculate how far away they were from the bridge because the Panzers were trying to take supplies to the German troops at the front of the of their lines. Yank put the glasses down and switched his view to the bridge far off to his left trying to calculate how far the Panzers had to go. The implications were clear that the Nazis had come to the end of their line.

Jean shook his head in awe, "The Germans are out of gas."

Yank handed the binoculars to Mikey who mournfully said, "Poor horses!"

"But Mikey," Jean said excitedly, "those poor horses are a sacrifice that will end the war for us."

Mikey shook his head, "I still think it's a shame."

Yank said, "But it's a necessary one. Horses' lives are saving human lives as they have been since the beginning of time."

After his near death experience in the jeep and getting a letter from his dad in the mail that they had picked up the night that scared him nearly to death, he felt a change come over him. He thought back on how he had had to give one of the members of the company now being sent to Stenay to guard the POWs a note about the response he had received from his dad saying, "Absolutely do not bring that French girl home." That broke his heart, but he felt he had to be honest with his beloved. He added in the postscript that he would try to come back and see her after the war was over if he could. He also thought about how precious every moment seemed to him after being so close to death. All his senses heightened, he enjoyed things that he had forgotten to notice like the intricate design of a snowflake as it fell onto his glove and the terrible sounds of the war around him especially anything having to do with gunfire, mortars, or just low flying planes strafing the land like the jeep's bullet holes holes penetrating the armor of the metal. Every sudden noise alarmed him internally and brought prickles to his skin. The smell of gunpowder tickled the insides of his nostrils and made his mouth dry. He felt for the first time since he had been in Europe that he was in harm's way.

After New Year's and the Christmas festivities, the letter he had received —all of these things made him ever more fully aware that something was going on out there that was way bigger than any of them knew and much more complex. He found himself sleeping less well, daydreaming more during the day, and picking up the ends of conversations only when a question was directed to him personally. His focus narrowed to wondering exactly where things were going on and why they never received any information until almost 24 hours after it had happened.

When his company got the news about the Massacre at Malmedy and how the Germans had simply and ruthlessly shot just any man who moved, he felt his fists tighten. Many of those American soldiers had not even been armed. How could Hitler and the Nazis be so brutal with human life? Those Allies who did not die from the stray bullets sprayed into the crowd, fumbling for cover froze to death in the cold. Some accounts said the Germans stripped the unsuspecting and luckless soldiers of all their ammunition and even of any clothing the Germans thought they could use.

Jean remembered some of the many talks he had had with the POWs and saw them as human beings. How desperate Hitler must be to gain back the land he had lost to tell his top aides to even sacrifice their own men to further the cause of the war. The entire company was in an uproar vowing to get revenge and more convinced than ever that the Third Reich needed to be wiped off the face of the world.

After listening to the bombs being dropped for what seemed like hours, Jean turned to Yank after a lull in the crashing, screeching whistles, and booming thuds of missiles landing everywhere. "Any famous last words if you don't make it?"

"Will you have your people contact my people?" Yank asked.

"You got it," Jean said. "Same here?"

"Yep," Yank replied.

With that, they dragged their bony butts off the hard brown ground, and lifted themselves to eye level with the edge of the trench, rifles ready, as they stared into the fiery red hell of the battle about to begin now that the bombing stopped.

EPILOGUE

Jean reached into his pocket to finger his good luck charm, the silver dollar his father had given him. He could neither find it nor face the battle without it. Much to Ernie's dismay, Jean crawled out of the trench to look for it in the nearby bushes where he had just squatted to answer a call of nature. Frantic but determined, he searched and searched until he found it. He returned to the foxhole to find it devastated and empty.

Just then, mortar fire hit the back of his helmet, and from nearby Ernie shouted at him to get down. He did, concussed with blood dripping down the back of his helmet. He was starting to beat himself up with survivor's guilt until Ernie explained that no one was hurt. They had all vacated the foxhole as soon as Jean left because they had guessed rightly it was no longer safe.

Jean trembled and concussed slowly drifted into a dreamlike state imagining himself back at his boyhood fishing hole with his pal. In a hazy way Jean pictured himself trying to catch a really big fish to bring to Merie and her family as a gift, but the fish kept eluding him. Olie Johnson was doing his part to cheer him up.

Then in the way of dreams, he shifted to walking with Ernie in the pebbled streams of the Ardennes now ruined by war. Ernie somehow knew he wanted to catch the fish of his life for Merie, but that was not to be. A fish whisked by, gave him a fishy wink and tugged at his line with an enticing stare only to escape death one more time. Jean lifted his rod, a pool cue, with his best lure noticing a beautiful woman suddenly behind him making nice to spur him on but to no avail. He lay down lazily as if to get into the mind of the fish who was eluding him. Ernie said, "You'd better let this one go too, Jean. I bet you can wrap your girl some nice little item from town and send that instead."

Later Jean wondered about the meaning of this dream vision... When he was just a boy, he had told Olie, 'Someday I am going to build a bridge." He had, in fact, realized that boyhood dream.

But his adult dream of strengthening his relationship with Merie had eluded him. He so wanted to sneak away on a mail run to Stenay, promise to love her and return for her someday. Unfortunately, he had other promises to keep. She surely was hurt by his letter telling her of his father's rejection. As he lay wounded on the battlefield, he felt the deeper ache in his heart that he had lost her forever.

AFTERWORD

Sue passed away before she could finish her book. She was most determined to at least summarize the rest of the story.

Jean survived the Battle of the Bulge and his Battalion advanced into the Rhineland where the 371st built the Wessel Bridge over a ten day period finishing it on April 9, 1945 and thereby allowing Allied troops to push the Nazis further into retreat.

Little is known of his final days in service. He may have liberated concentration camps and seen sights that should remain unseen.

Upon his return, he kept in touch with only one war buddy Jack Pemberton of Kewanee, a nearby town. Otherwise he maintained a cordial but distant relationship with those who reminded him of war. Most assuredly he suffered from undiagnosed PTSD.

He took a job working nights at J.I. Case operating a forklift and moved back in with his parents contributing to their finances. He married Rose Marie Langdon, moved into a newly constructed home in west Rock Island built by the family carpenters, and rapidly welcomed three daughters.

His wife struggled with undiagnosed postpartum depression and was unable to adequately care for their three little girls under age three while Jean worked nights and slept days. One night, Rose took his lucky silver dollar and used it to buy a beer. Jean could forgive almost anything, but he lost it over this. Jean compensated for the loss of his good luck charm by wearing his St. Christopher medal around his neck. He noticed he liked the weight of it and the warmth of it in sunlight. He wondered if maybe it was St. Christopher who had protected him.

The couple eventually divorced, and Rose gave up custody of the children. Jean took over as a single father. He never remarried and though they were legally divorced, he sometimes supported Rose when needed and even contributed to her funeral. He believed they were still married in the eyes of the Church.

Jean's portrait painted by the Belgian street artist

Jean's rosary and medal

Jean's European Campaign and Good Conduct Medals

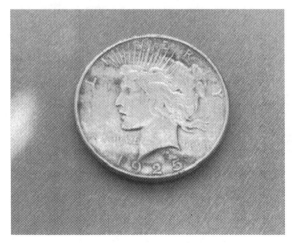

A Liberty Silver Dollar minted the year of Jean's
birth in 1925. This is similar to the one that his
father gave him for luck and protection.

Jean's Army Ring.

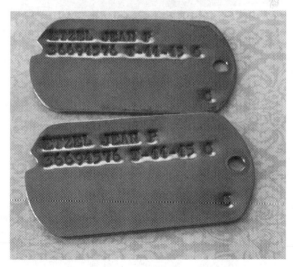

Jean's dog tags.

Jean with his three daughters. Sue is
the smiling one on the right.

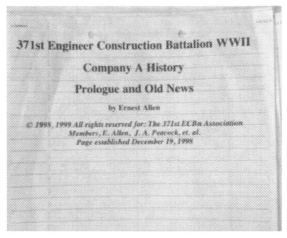

371st Engineer Construction Battalion WWII

Company A History

Prologue and Old News

by Ernest Allen

© 1998, 1999 All rights reserved for: The 371st ECBn Association
Members, E. Allen, J. A. Peacock, et. al.
Page established December 19, 1998

The cover of Lieutenant Ernie Allen's narrative
frequently referred to in the text.

A St. Christopher Medal similar to the one Jean's mom
gave him for his safety and protection in battle.

PFC Jean P. Etzel

A horse pulling a German tank through the Ardennes.

Jean with his daughters and friends.

Jean in later life.

Jean with his family.

Jean in civilian life

Printed in the United States
by Baker & Taylor Publisher Services